K-Directorate was also cold. *Cold enough to see my breath,* Sydney thought, exhaling. She shivered as she followed Diana down the halls.

Diana stopped at a small kitchen jutting off from the east wing. "Orientation starts in an hour," she said. "We'll make sure you get a good seat. Just remember—"

Another woman entered the kitchen, cutting off Diana's last piece of advice. Her mouth turned up in a half smile. "Diana, is this your new recruit?"

"Sasha Petrova," Diana said, stepping back as Sydney smiled brightly, "meet Anna Espinosa."

ALIAS™

INFILTRATION

BREEN FRAZIER

AN ORIGINAL PREQUEL NOVEL BASED ON THE
HIT TV SERIES CREATED BY J. J. ABRAMS

BANTAM BOOKS
NEW YORK ✳ TORONTO ✳ LONDON ✳ SYDNEY ✳ AUCKLAND

Alias: Infiltration

A Bantam Book / May 2004
Text and cover art copyright © 2004 by Touchstone Television

ISBN: 0-553-49437-6

Visit us on the Web! www.randomhouse.com

Published simultaneously in the United States and Canada

Bantam Books is an imprint of Random House Children's Books, a
division of Random House, Inc. BANTAM BOOKS and the rooster
colophon are registered trademarks of Random House, Inc.

PRINTED IN THE UNITED STATES OF AMERICA

OPM 10 9 8 7 6 5 4 3 2

ALIAS™

INFILTRATION

1

"DON'T JUDGE." FRANCIE SAID, turning off the lights, "until you get the full effect."

Sydney Bristow wasn't sure what she was looking at. Then her eyes adjusted to the sudden darkness of the summer evening and she noticed a luminescent glow coming from the ceiling.

Stars. Neon green glow-in-the-dark stars.

"You always talk about how you can never see the stars in L.A.," Francie said, smiling. "Not like you could in West Virginia, anyway. So . . . voilà! What do you think?"

Her roommate had done an impressive job,

Sydney couldn't deny it. Francie Calfo had hung up constellations, nebulae, even a spaceship with an alien waving from the cockpit.

"I love it," Sydney said. "But it seems like a lot of work for something temporary." At least, she hoped it was temporary.

"Not really," Francie replied. "It just took a few minutes to stick them on. It's summer now. . . . We can have a little fun."

Sydney and Francie had finished freshman year classes at UCLA with a whimper instead of a bang. Sydney had stayed up for seventy-two hours straight cramming for finals, trying to catch up on all the lectures she'd missed as a result of her job. The only outlet she had allowed herself was buying a Super Soaker and chasing Francie up and down the halls of the dorm. Francie had responded by buying one of her own.

"You're insane, you know that?" Francie had asked Sydney one night as they dried their clothes and Sydney went back to studying. "You wouldn't even be in this situation if it weren't for that stupid bank."

Sydney hadn't responded. She couldn't explain to Francie that she didn't work at a bank—she was an agent for SD-6, a secret branch of the CIA. And when the CIA said you had to go to work, you skipped your classes. Period.

* * *

Sydney still couldn't believe how she had stumbled into this life. Nor could she believe how many life-threatening situations she had survived. But the trade-off for such eye-opening experiences had been another kind of education, not only in the world of intelligence, but also in the cynical world of human behavior. Sydney had discovered that good spies weren't necessarily loyal spies. She'd found out that your superiors were just as likely to sell you out as enemy agents were. And she'd decided that there was only one man she knew she could always trust: Arvin Sloane.

The director of operations at SD-6, Arvin Sloane radiated trust and confidence. He took every mission, every risk, seriously. More importantly, he took *Sydney* seriously. At first, Sydney had had trouble understanding why she put so much faith in Sloane. Then she had realized that it was simply because he listened.

He listened. To *her*.

As the youngest field agent at SD-6—and the

youngest employee the agency had ever taken on—
Sydney felt she was being judged at all times. Her coworkers, particularly the men whose careers had
stalled because of missions that had gone south, made
sure she felt their disdain, like a weight on her shoulders. *What are you doing here?* their eyes seemed to
say. *This isn't the place for you, little girl.*

But Sloane was different. He believed in her. He
seemed genuinely interested in what she had to say.
Once, when he had asked her how she liked working
at SD-6, Sydney had babbled on for five minutes
about how the organization inspired in her a patriot-
ism she never knew she had. *Shut up, shut up, you're
making a fool of yourself in front of your boss,* she'd
told herself, and then ended her speech with a self-
deprecating "But don't listen to me, I'm just the new
kid," expecting Sloane to politely turn the conversation to something else. Instead, an odd light had shone
in his eyes, and he had grabbed one of her hands with
both of his. "Don't think that, Sydney," he'd told her,
his voice shaking with emotion. "Don't ever think
that. This organization was built by people like you.
Passionate people who believe in our cause. If I had
ten agents like you, we could take over the world."

That had been the moment that Sydney had realized she would die for him.

Which was why she'd listened in May when

Sloane had instructed her not to take summer classes, even though a few now would have lightened her burden in the fall. And when he'd said, "Nothing out of the ordinary, I just need you to be available for a mission. It's standard operating procedure," she had waited. And waited. Sloane had termed it indefinite standby, but after weeks of waiting Sydney had been convinced she was about to be fired.

Eventually her fears melted away. In June she had traveled to Niagara Falls for a mission as well as bonding course with her fellow SD agents—and the shock of learning that one of them was a double agent had made her grateful to have a break. Before she knew it, it was mid July, and she found herself on a steady diet of sleep—eight hours a night, for a change—yoga, and bad summer movies. She had forgotten the bliss of the pure vegetative state.

Of course, Sydney wouldn't have minded sharing that bliss with someone. Francie was still spending most of her time at her summer nanny gig—she'd spent several weeks in New Mexico with her young charges. Now she was back, but Sydney had barely seen her. That made what was happening with Noah, her sometimes boyfriend, even more frustrating.

While Sydney was sitting on the sidelines waiting for her mission, Noah Hicks seemed to be doing double duty at SD-6. She knew he loved being in the field, and the last thing she wanted to do was make him feel guilty for not paying enough attention to her. But it bothered her that his idea of spending time together was talking for five minutes on a secure sat-phone once a week, if she was lucky. She wasn't even sure where they stood. Was he her boyfriend? Or were they just dating?

"Let's call it dating plus," Noah had said when she'd tried to pin him down.

"Plus what?" she'd asked. But he'd danced his way around that one, leaving her to wonder.

And now, as Sydney stared at Francie's stars glowing on the ceiling, she wondered if she could afford to have a little fun.

* * *

When the clock says 2:30 a.m., it's time to stop lying to yourself, Sydney decided.

Eight hours of sleep a night? More like four hours of tossing and turning and four of actual sleep.

Yoga? She'd hated it. Quit after three sessions.

Bad summer movies? They were just that—bad.

And Noah? Well, the Noah situation did bother her. But that wasn't what kept her awake at night. It wasn't what made her get out of bed and take long walks around campus. It wasn't what made her Krav

Maga sparring partner stop her in the middle of a round and ask, "What are you taking out on *me*?"

Sydney was *restless*.

Field agents talked about this all the time, how you could never get the high in your normal life that you felt on missions. She was missing that high, missing the rush. But somehow, that didn't quite cover it. What Sydney felt was deeper; it reached deep into her soul and shook her. It was . . .

It was . . . a voice.

The revelation had come in a routine SD-6 psych evaluation. Dr. Eisendrath had leaned forward and asked, "Are you hearing voices yet?"

She had been so startled, she'd almost dropped her tea.

Dr. Eisendrath had laughed. "It happens to most agents," he'd said. "Part of the conditioning you build for yourself in life-threatening scenarios."

"Is it bad?"

"Not at all," he had replied. "Nine times out of ten, it will save your life."

Dr. Eisendrath had been right—the voice had saved her life. It was the voice that had said, *Grab the extra clip for the gun!* or, *There's someone behind that door!* Sydney had told herself that the voice came from the part of her brain where training overlapped with instinct.

He'd refilled her cup. "What's important," he had added, brewing another pot of tea, "is that you figure out who that voice is."

"What do you mean?" she had asked. "It's *me*."

"Maybe," he had said, raising an eyebrow. "Let's talk about your mother some more."

Sydney had understood what Dr. Eisendrath had been getting at, that the voice was a manifestation of some other presence in her life. She just couldn't accept it. She was Sydney Bristow. No one spoke for her.

The bizarre thing was, the voice had been coming out during odd moments lately, non-life-threatening moments. And while it didn't bother her, she couldn't help wondering what it meant.

Perhaps, Sydney, you're overthinking it.

Perhaps. Or perhaps there was a part of her that missed risking her life, that missed hearing the voice. But that was crazy, wasn't it?

Not necessarily.

Sydney turned on the television. Settling in for a long night of insomnia, she drew some small comfort from the company of Insane Eddie, who told her his prices were so low, he was practically *giving* things away.

Now *that* guy was crazy.

2

NOAH HAD ONCE TOLD Sydney, "I care for you every bit as much as you care for me. It just comes out differently, that's all."

"What does that mean?" she'd demanded. It had sounded vaguely insulting.

"It means I have trouble showing affection the way you do. But that doesn't mean it's not there."

Sydney had tried to rationalize this a hundred different ways, but it had never made sense. She'd thought about it while she'd sat awake with only Insane Eddie to distract her, and it still hadn't made sense. But that morning, when she caught Noah stepping off the elevator, surrounded by eight SD-6 agents simultaneously debriefing him, she suddenly understood what he meant.

The moment their eyes met, she broke into a ridiculous grin. It was too big, too toothy. Anyone who saw them just then would instantly realize they were "dating plus." Noah gave her a half grin in reply, all he had time for before the debriefers whisked him into Sloane's office. Sydney didn't feel rejected. That half grin hid a bigger one for later.

It just comes out differently, that's all.

To get that, you had to get Noah.

He caught up with her later, in the copy room.

"How was Kyoto?" she asked.

"Crowded," he replied. "But we stopped some loose nukes. What'd you do this weekend?"

"Caught a James Bond movie marathon."

"Sounds like you had more fun."

"What happened with the nukes?"

"We shipped the cores back here to the States and the bomb casings to Moscow." Sydney looked at him in alarm. Nuclear bomb casings could easily fall into the wrong hands in post–Cold War Russia.

"We made sure they ended up in the right hands," he added, seeming to read her mind.

She was walking back to her desk when he steered her into the conference room.

"C'mere," he whispered. "There's something I need to tell you."

The room was empty and the lights were low. The sensation of his breath on her ear, his hand on her elbow, was enough to make her head spin. She'd had fantasies of ducking into a closet with him. . . . It was stupid, stupid, stupid. But she couldn't stop her mind from going to that place sometimes.

"What's going on?" she whispered back.

"Sydney." The voice was Arvin Sloane's. Sydney turned, startled. She'd been caught. Had he been there the whole time, or had he just walked in? More importantly, did he suspect what she was thinking? But Sloane had another agenda.

"Sorry for the cloak-and-dagger. This is an emergency briefing."

Noah held out her chair for her. *Just wait,* his face assured her, *this is gonna be good.*

Sloane folded his hands. "I know you've been wondering why you haven't gone on any missions recently."

Sydney nodded.

"The reason," Sloane said, "is that we've been waiting for Agent Hicks to put the last piece into place."

Her eyes shifted to Noah, who sat beside her. "The nuke casings I sent to Moscow were used to help buy cover for an SD-9 agent acting as a mole," he said.

"Who's the agent?" Sydney asked.

"We don't know his identity," Noah said. "SD-9 is playing it close to the vest to protect him."

"Fortunately," Sloane added, "the plan worked. And this SD-9 double agent has just been promoted to the rank of handler."

"Handler" was an intelligence term. Which meant the mole worked for an intelligence organization like SD-6. And there was only one of those in Moscow.

"K-Directorate," Sydney said, her eyes wide. "You're talking about K-Directorate."

"That's right," Sloane murmured. Sydney turned to Noah again, making sure this was for real. *I told you this would be good,* his smile said.

"What does this have to do with me?"

"As a handler, our guy has discretion over a certain number of low-ranking officers and field agents," Noah said. "We think this is a perfect time to sneak in another double."

"We want to send you," Sloane said.

Sydney blinked.

"Me?" she said, her voice cracking.

"Your job is simple," Sloane said. "We need you to download a virus onto K-Directorate's computer network. It will allow us complete access to their infrastructure. Once we have a better understanding of that, we'll be able to assess whether the rumors are true."

Sydney didn't have to ask which rumors those were. Directorate-K was a former branch of the KGB. It had kept tabs on foreign agents both abroad and inside the Soviet Union. But when the Communist regime fell and the U.S.S.R. dissolved, the KGB had been reborn the SVR, and Directorate-K had become K-Directorate.

These seemingly minor changes had sent tremors through the intelligence community around the world. The SVR, struggling to maintain relevance in an increasingly democratic society, had promised that its era of eavesdropping on innocent civilians would come to an end. Russians, they promised, would live in a truly free society.

K-Directorate was supposed to play by the rules. But as democracy failed to relieve economic hardship and black markets thrived, K-Directorate had become less and less open. And then, in May, twelve SVR agents had been killed, gangland-style. No one had claimed credit. The murders had never been solved. But the rumor mill had exploded.

And the rumor mill said K-Directorate had gone rogue.

They no longer operated under any authority except

their own. And yet, because the organization had at one time been associated with Russian intelligence, they had the perfect cover. They could still claim they were legitimate, even though they devoted every ounce of their power to freelance intelligence work.

For Sydney, this mission would mean exposing the truth about K-Directorate, giving SD-6 the silver bullet they needed to bring this rogue down.

It was amazing that Sloane would put this much trust in her.

It was a stupendous opportunity.

And it didn't make a lick of sense.

"Wait a minute," Sydney said slowly. "With all due respect, why me? We have dozens of agents with more deep-cover experience."

"Yes," Sloane said. "But none fills the bill quite as well as you do. You're exactly what K-Directorate is looking for."

That was a compliment. She guessed.

Sloane leaned forward. "SD-6 recruited you because you fit a certain profile. Not surprisingly, K-Directorate looks for the same qualities in their agents. Loyalty. Intelligence. Healthy suspicion of authority on a national level. You also have an innate ability to engender trust in everyone you meet." He paused. "People want to believe you, Sydney. That's a rare gift in our field."

"Not to mention," Noah added, "that your Russian is amazing." This was true. Of all the languages she'd mastered at SD-6, Russian had come to her the fastest. The Romance languages had been easy, since they were all Latin-based and shared most of the same roots. But the kanji characters of Japanese took an impossible amount of concentration to remember. Once she threw Cantonese and Mandarin into the mix, it was impossible to keep all the Oriental languages straight. Russian, however, was different. The Cyrillic alphabet just came naturally to her. There were even lessons where she was *ahead* of her SD-6 tutor.

"So all I have to do," Sydney asked, "is download a virus?"

"That's the easy part," Noah smirked. "The hard part's getting through the vetting process."

"K-Directorate will investigate every nook and cranny of your alias," Sloane said. "They will test you. They will lie to you. They'll try to get you to contradict yourself, and you won't even notice."

"Every conversation you have," Noah said, "will be analyzed, parsed, and deconstructed. Do you say hi to the cleaning staff? Are you friendly with your coworkers or standoffish? Do you like croutons on your salad?"

"What if I like soup?"

"It will be two weeks before you're granted network privileges," Sloane continued, "during which time you will be in greater danger than you've ever been in."

He pressed a button by his desk, displaying a picture on the monitors. "To help you pass this stage, your first priority when you land in Moscow is to meet this man."

Sydney took in the picture of a grizzled man about sixty years old with sunken eyes and permanent frown lines. "This is Anatoly Gromnovich," Sloane explained. "Retired SD-9, Russian expatriate who took up residence again after Communism crumbled."

"Retired?" Sydney prompted. How much help could the guy be if he wasn't in the game anymore?

"He's still the world's foremost identity expert. The profile he sets up for you should be unassailable. The trade-off is that you won't have much time to learn the details of your alias. Once K-Directorate brings you in, there's no turning back until we get you back home."

"How long will I be in the field?" Sydney asked.

"Six weeks," Sloane replied. "*That's* why I didn't want you taking any summer courses."

Six weeks would put her back at UCLA right before classes began.

Sloane noticed she'd fallen silent. "Is there a problem with that?"

"No. No, of course not."

Sloane stood and took the other seat next to her. "Sydney, listen to me," he said. "I understand that it's frightening, SD-6 placing this amount of responsibility on your shoulders. But look at all you've accomplished since you've been with us. We considered sending Agent Hicks with you—"

"I lobbied for it," Noah interrupted.

Sloane barely noticed. "But we felt that you excel on solo missions where you're allowed to come up with your own solutions in high-pressure scenarios." His hand reached out and pressed hers. "This is what you were *meant* to do. I believe that."

Sloane's words always had a calming effect on her. "I just hope I don't let you down," she said.

Sloane smiled, touched. "That's not possible. You're going to make an incredible double agent."

3

THIS IS WHAT SYDNEY knew about Graham Flinkman, head of technical services at SD-6:

He was furiously neat.

He liked trains, but the idea of a model train set was abhorrent.

He could name all fifty state capitals, but only if he sang the "Animaniacs" song that rhymed that information.

He was not named after the graham cracker, nor was the graham cracker named after him. Why anyone would ever make either of these assumptions was a mystery to Sydney. But for some reason, he insisted on explaining that to everyone he met.

And he was a genius.

Sydney had met fewer than five such people in her life, people who transcended what was normally perceived as intelligent and entered a realm where average human beings couldn't follow. The idea that a three-wheeled car was more stable than a four-wheeled one was common sense to someone like Graham. That he would spend three sleepless weeks proving it, and vindicate himself with a patent that was immediately bought up and squashed by a major automobile company since it would bankrupt Detroit, was typical behavior.

Graham didn't really care. He wasn't interested in money. But the incident helped Sydney understand him better. To him, the only real conundrum in life was why more people didn't see the world the way he did.

So when Sydney entered his office, she wasn't taken aback when he sang to her, "Sydney! Sydney Brisbane!" It threw her for a second until she put it together: Sydney . . . Brisbane . . . Both cities in Australia.

"How are you, Graham?"

"Good, good. Here for your op-tech, I take it."

"What have you cooked up for me?"

He held up his index finger. "See this?"

"Your finger?"

"No, *this*." He held it closer.

"Your fingerprint?"

"No," he insisted. *"This."* His finger was practically touching her eyeball.

"Graham, why don't you tell me what I'm supposed to be looking at?"

He carefully peeled off his own skin from his fingertip. When he held it up for Sydney, she saw that it was a thin latex strip that seamlessly adhered to his finger.

"Not bad," she said. "What does it do?"

Graham sat her in front of a computer. "You know how when you log on, SD-6 has you enter your name and password?"

"Yeah?"

"Well, K-Directorate's taken that one step further. Check out the mouse."

There was a detachable plastic sleeve on top of it. "What is it?"

"It's a biometric scanner. Reads your fingerprint."

Sydney stuck her finger under the sleeve and felt a light tingling sensation. On the computer monitor, an ID screen appeared. It included her SD-6 badge photo and a name.

"Sasha Petrova?" she asked, reading aloud.

"It's the only thing SD-9 would share about your alias."

Sydney rolled the name over in her brain, getting used to it. *Sasha Petrova, Sasha Petrova, Sasha Petrova.*

"The mole inside K-Directorate was also able to give us their system specs," Graham added. "Which is how I found out about the fingerprint scanner. That's why you're gonna need the fake fingerprint."

She stared at him, confused. He'd skipped a step, which was typical for Graham. "Why am I going to need it again?"

"Uh, hello? Because the virus is twenty-five megs." This was also typical for Graham. He made you feel stupid for not making the connections he did, even though he freely admitted he had trouble balancing his checkbook.

"That's a lot?"

"That's huge. The moment you download it, K-Directorate's gonna be all, 'Huh? What? Who's doing that? Petrova, is that you?' And you'll be all, 'Me? Working for the CIA? Never.' And they'll be all, 'Well, why don't you come onto this firing range and put this blindfold on and we'll play target practice—' "

"Okay, I get it," she said impatiently. "So with your latex fake, I can pretend I'm somebody else."

"Exactly," he said. "But first you have to *get* that

somebody else's fingerprint. Which you do like so. . . ." He grabbed a new fake, this one blank. He peeled off the adhesive and stuck it onto her finger. Then he took his own finger and pressed it firmly against hers.

"You have to hold it for eight seconds," he explained.

"Eight seconds?"

"Eight seconds."

"Eight seconds is a long time for something like this."

"Any less and you'll only get a partial print." He pulled his right index finger away and held it next to hers. They were exactly the same.

"Now check this out," he said, slipping her finger back onto the mouse. The screen replaced her image with his. The name changed from SASHA PETROVA to GRAHAM (NOT THE CRACKER) FLINKMAN.

He pulled the chair back and escorted her to a large lab table in the middle of his workspace. "Now," he said, "because HYDRA's so big—"

"What's HYDRA?"

"The virus you're downloading."

"Oh. Like the myth."

"The what?"

"The myth. You know, the multiheaded monster? You cut off one head and six more sprout out of it?"

He stared at her as if she were insane. "Uh, no. It stands for Hardcore Young Double Agent's Reconnaissance Assignment. That's you."

Sydney let that one go.

"Anyway, since HYDRA's so big, you're gonna need a five-minute window to download it. Hence, these goodies." He offered her a pen.

"What does it do?" she asked, clicking it. On the second click, a three-inch hypodermic needle shot from the tip.

"That," Graham replied. He gently took the pen from her and unscrewed the casing. Inside was an ink cartridge and a thin syringe filled with a clear liquid. "One hundred cc's of Scopolamine, GHB, and horse tranquilizer. Anything smaller than a rhino is out for fifteen minutes. Not to mention it wipes your short-term memory clean. Even if they see you coming, they won't remember it when they wake up."

"Really?" she asked skeptically. Those types of drugs were notoriously unreliable.

"I tested it on myself, and I don't remember last *week*." He handed her a phone. "Next up is this bad boy. It's your standard SD-6 phone. But enter the right combination and . . ." He trailed off, punching ten numbers into the phone, followed by the pound sign. Two needles shot from the phone into his desk.

Electric currents ran down the wires that still attached the phone to the needles, charring the wood on his desk to a crisp black.

"It's a Taser." Sydney nodded appreciatively, waving her hand in front of her face to remove the smell of burned oak.

"Thirty thousand volts. Definitely enough to knock somebody out."

Sydney studied him. "How many times have you shot yourself?"

"Four or five," he replied without hesitation. "Your skin gets kind of numb to it after three."

* * *

When she got back to her desk, a mountain of paperwork waited for her. This was typical SD-6 protocol. You were assigned to a top-secret, hush-hush mission—and yet somehow, somebody knew where you were going, because the plane, hotel, and rental car were already booked. Sydney knew there were whole SD-6 departments devoted to these details. She'd never met anyone from them, but she'd talked to several unpleasant people from accounting on the phone. They tracked her traveling expenses like hawks. Thus, she was not surprised to see that the top memo was a reminder not to watch the in-flight movie. Or at least not to expect SD-6 to pay for it.

Noah appeared over her desk. "Don't tell me you're not excited about this," he said.

She glanced up. "I am."

"Well, you don't look it."

"I guess I get bummed out when I read"—she ran her finger under the release she was signing— " 'The CIA is not responsible for the retrieval of your remains in the instance of any fatality that might lead to agency compromise.' "

Noah pulled up a chair beside her. "That's not going to happen. Do you think I would have been the first to recommend you to Sloane for this job if I thought it might?"

Sydney's pen tore through the release. "You recommended me?"

"Only from the moment we heard we could sneak somebody inside K-Directorate." He shook his head, surprised she hadn't figured it out yet. "Do you think I liked being away from you this past month? Sydney, the whole reason I've been gone—it's all been for you."

Sydney didn't know what to say.

* * *

On their fourth official date, Noah had packed a picnic basket and a blanket and taken her to a closed section of Griffith Park. They'd sat on a rock outcropping that allowed for a perfect view of the entire park, the Hollywood sign, and the twinkling city lights in the distance. As incredible as the setting had been, she was unprepared for what came next. He'd held her close and *made* her talk. "I have a hundred questions for you," he had whispered in her ear. "And I want to know everything."

All her life, Sydney had tried to make herself disappear. To avoid being the center of attention. But that day, she had sat with someone who wouldn't let her do that. Noah had challenged her. Teased her. Made her justify what she stood for. And once Sydney had accepted that she wouldn't be laughed at or judged, the floodgates had opened. She'd revealed more to him on one date than she had to Francie all year. She'd talked about her father, about the death of her mother, about everything else they could think of. And not only heavy stuff like politics and moral issues—though she loved sparring with him. Topics had ranged from the goofy to the intimate. And maybe they hadn't all been as deep as talking about Proust, but there'd been a giddy thrill to snuggling close to somebody and saying "I *really* love Cap'n Crunch" only to hear "So do I" in response.

As wonderful as the day had been, Sydney had been troubled that Noah seemed to have some agenda. He was seeking *something,* she realized after they'd sat talking about her for six hours straight. But no matter how hard she'd tried, she couldn't get him to open up in return.

"What about you?" she had asked. "Who's the great love of your life?"

"We're not done talking about you yet," he'd replied. "So if you want to be an English teacher, what are you doing at SD-6?"

She had thought about that and said, "I'm *going* to be an English teacher. But there's a part of me that wants the deep-cover field rating. I *want* that clearance. I *want* to know what's going on in the world. And I want to make it a safer place."

She'd stopped, hearing the words that had just come out of her mouth, and cradled her head in her hands. She had been convinced she had uttered the biggest cliché in the book.

By that point in the evening, she'd been wrapped in his arms, which were in turn wrapped in the blanket. He'd rested his chin on her shoulder. "You're going to get all that and more. But after you do, don't be surprised if you'd still rather be an English teacher."

* * *

Now, as he stared at her over her desk at SD-6, Noah asked, "Isn't this what you wanted? To go on deep-cover missions like this?"

Part of her was incredibly moved and wanted to thank him. This mission would be a boon to her advancement inside SD-6. But there was another part of her that wanted to tell him, *It's not what I wanted from* you. *I want you here, with me. I don't want you halfway around the world, setting up missions for me. I want you to pick up the phone when I call. I want you to listen when I've had a bad day.* The disconnect scared her. One moment, he was holding her close in a gorgeous park, hanging on her every word. The next he was staring at her blankly, while she almost burst into tears trying to explain something.

Sometimes they felt like soul mates.

Sometimes they felt like strangers.

Sometimes on the same date.

"It *is* what I want," she said. And since this wasn't the place to dissect the issues of their relationship, she added, "It's just . . . I don't know how Francie's going to take it."

Noah bought it. "You've told me a lot about her," he said. "And if she's half the friend you say she is, she'll understand." He discreetly but affectionately squeezed her shoulder. "The people who love you always do."

Then he left.

* * *

"Six weeks?" Francie cried, watching Sydney throw a summer's worth of clothes into a suitcase.

"It won't be that long," Sydney said, not buying her own lie.

Neither did Francie. "Of course not. It's only, oh, the whole *summer*."

Sydney took a deep breath. "Francie, the bank has offered me this incredible internship experience. . . . It just happens to be in the Boston office. How can I say no? " She was ready to launch into the many further excuses she'd come up with. But when she turned around, Francie was slamming the bathroom door behind her.

Sydney waited for five minutes before she knocked. "Francie . . . ?"

"Go *away*," Francie ordered. Her voice was muffled.

"I'm coming in."

"If you do, I'll hate you forever."

"You already hate me. I made you clean the

bathroom last week, remember?" Sydney jumped back as Francie suddenly opened the door, went to her bed, and flopped down into the fetal position, with her face buried in her pillow.

This was new. The fetal position was definitely new.

"Don't sit down," Francie warned as Sydney sat down. "And don't touch me," Francie said, shrinking away as Sydney's hand found her shoulder.

Sydney said nothing. If she started, Francie would have an opening to attack. So they sat in silence for a few seconds until Francie got up and began rooting through her closet. "I'm so stupid," Francie said, sniffling. "I thought I had my best friend back."

"Francie, c'mon—"

"C'mon *what*?" Francie cut her off. "Face facts, Syd, it's not like we've been close the past few months."

She started to go through her shoe tree, pulling off shoes she'd always hated and throwing them into the corner. This wasn't a good sign, either. When Francie had something difficult to say to someone, such as *I'm breaking up with you* or *Can you lend me some money?* she couldn't look them in the eye.

"I mean, it's not a bad thing. It's what people do, right?" She finished with her shoes and began attacking her wardrobe. Then, talking into a red sleeveless blouse, she said, "You're a loner, Syd. You don't need friends."

"That's not true!" Sydney protested.

"Then why do you keep pushing me away?" Francie asked the blouse as she hung it back up. The blouse never knew how close it had come to being executed. "Maybe we shouldn't be roommates next year."

Sydney's heart sank to her stomach. This wasn't a regular fight at all. This was the real thing.

Sydney bounced off the bed and spun Francie around. "Look," she said, digging into her pockets. "Look."

She pulled out a bag of glow-in-the-dark stars. "I'm going to take these with me. And I'll put them up wherever I'm staying. And every night, when I'm falling asleep, I'll stare at them and think of you."

But that wasn't enough. Francie's face didn't change.

Sydney wrapped her roommate in a fierce hug. "I will always be your friend. That's never going to change."

"Yeah," Francie muttered. Not sarcasm, exactly, but disbelief. She said yeah, but what she meant was *Things won't be different when you come back. And you know it.*

K-DIRECTORATE CONTROLLED THE entire closed-circuit surveillance network that covered Moscow, a system of over twenty-four hundred cameras. Half were in public areas, the other half posted in the hallways, apartment buildings, and houses of the unsuspecting.

And since these cameras dotted the urban landscape, SD-9 had a difficult time finding Sydney an unwatched apartment to stay in for an extended period of time. The unhappy solution was a flat in the worst part of Moscow, on the block where you wouldn't let your armed bodyguard walk alone at night. Her first clue to how bad it was came when her taxi driver dropped her off at the address, refused to help her with her bags, and sped away as soon as she slammed the trunk.

The air reeked of garbage, due to the presence of a city dump less than two miles away. As the setting sun cut through the haze, Sydney could see particles of refuse floating in the air. She dodged homeless men, women, and children—a lot of children—who saw a moderately well-dressed young woman as a target.

"Some change?" they begged. "Bite to eat?" "Have the time?" The last request, she knew, was a ploy to make her check her wrist while they picked her pocket.

The lock to the security door was broken, so Sydney pushed her way into the building. She stopped at a dead drop along the way to pick up the key to the flat since SD-6 had told her the landlord was an unreliable drunk. The broken elevator wasn't a surprise, nor was the dark water dripping from the ceiling. But the state of disrepair inside her apartment still caught her by surprise when she pushed open the door.

The odor assaulted her first, an unpleasant mixture of formaldehyde and bleach and whatever cleansing agents the previous occupant had used to hose down the space. But it wasn't enough to cover up the smell, which Sydney placed immediately. It was the smell of death.

When she swung open her bedroom closet, she found the source. Dark brown spots had seeped into the rotting paneling, and stench wafted out as if she had just opened a crypt.

I don't think I can live here, she thought.

But some part of her said, *Yes, you can.*

The size wasn't too bad. It was roughly as big as her UCLA dorm room—meaning that two steps from the middle of the flat in any direction would get her wherever she needed to go: the bathroom, the kitchen, the bedroom. The only piece of furniture in the room was a chair, which rested in front of the only window.

The last tenant had been kind enough to leave a broom wedged between the refrigerator and stove. Its bristles were worn and filthy, which was odd because the kitchen was littered with lost bites of food, cigarette butts, and . . .

And rats.

The apartment had rats.

"Hello!" a cheerful voice called from the hallway. Sydney turned to see a woman of about fifty, kitchen pot in hand, standing at her door. "You must be the university student."

"Sasha," Sydney said.

"Maryam Andropov," the woman said. "I see you've discovered the morgue."

"Excuse me?" she said in perfect Russian.

"A month and a half ago, the police raided this apartment. They didn't make any arrests, but they found three bodies stuffed in your closet."

That explained the smell, at least. Evidently SD-9 had rented an apartment owned by a serial killer. This mission was not getting off to a good start.

"What are you cooking? It smells delicious." Actually, it smelled like dirty feet. But it was an improvement over her apartment.

"Potato vareniki," the woman said, lifting the lid. Sydney saw potatoes, beets, and cabbage reduced to a leathery stew. "Come, you must have dinner with Samson and me."

"Samson?"

"My husband. I insist. I always cook for the new tenants, and I don't take no for an answer!"

* * *

Sydney Bristow had faced down gun barrels. She'd bested men who were twice her size in physical combat. She'd played mind games with agents who could beat Deep Blue at a game of chess. But nothing prepared her for the sheer force of will that was Maryam Andropov.

"The thing you have to understand," she explained to Sydney, "is that I *know* I'm crazy. My Samson tells me so all the time."

"I don't need that much," Sydney said. Mrs. Andropov had been scooping vareniki onto her plate since she stepped into the apartment.

"Well, who else is going to eat it?" Mrs. Andropov asked, anguished. "Besides, it's Samson's favorite. You'll hurt his feelings if you don't tell him how much you love it. Now sit. You make me nervous when you stand."

The couch appeared innocent enough. But when she sat, Sydney found herself sinking deeper and deeper. The pillows on top were merely a cover for softer pillows underneath, which sucked her in like a Venus flytrap and made escape impossible.

Mrs. Andropov's apartment was twice the size of Sydney's, and well kept. The more Sydney inspected it, the more she doubted that any male existed in it.

"Uh . . . where *is* your husband?" Sydney asked.

"Over there," Mrs. Andropov replied, pointing her ladle. Sydney followed the ladle with her eyes to an urn resting on the mantel above the fireplace.

Sydney felt awkward that she'd even asked. "I . . . I'm sorry," she said. Mrs. Andropov shoved the heaping plate of food into her chest with a shrug. Inexplicably, Sydney sank deeper into the cushions. Her backbone touched the base of the couch, where what felt like decades of loose change, earrings, and pairs of glasses dug into her spine. *I wonder if the serial killer hid his extra bodies here,* Sydney thought.

"What do you have to be sorry about?" Mrs. Andropov demanded. "I'm the one who still talks to her dead husband. All right, let's say grace."

Mrs. Andropov held the plate out like an offering. "Samson, please watch over this strange girl and keep her safe."

Amen, Sydney thought.

"Also," Mrs. Andropov said, "please talk to God and fix it so my cooking doesn't give her gas the way it always did you." She clanked her fork on the plate. "Dig in."

Sydney tentatively scooped a forkful of the food into her mouth. It was surprisingly good.

"It's tough being alone," Mrs. Andropov sniffed. "You get so used to cooking for two. I always end up throwing half of it out. My Samson keeps asking me, 'Woman, why do you waste so much?' And I say, 'Shut up, Samson, you're dead.' But if I didn't have him to talk to, I'd go crazy, I guess. Good thing you showed up. What're you doing tomorrow night? Do you know how to play pinochle?"

"Working," Sydney replied a little too quickly. But the woman didn't mean any harm. She just wanted some company after who knew how many years alone. When Sydney's gaze fell on an old black-and-white photograph, her heart went out to Mrs. Andropov.

In the picture, a young, slender bride, obviously Mrs. Andropov, walked out of a church with her Samson on her arm. A crowd surrounded the newlyweds, but her husband was pulling her close, whispering in her ear something so amusing that she had thrown her head back in gales of laughter when the picture had been snapped. The woman in the picture was vibrant and full of life, ready to take on the world with her husband by her side. Not like this lonely figure standing before Sydney, reduced to feeding hungry college students as an excuse to talk.

"So where are you from, strange girl?" Mrs. Andropov asked.

Sydney had no idea how to respond. She hadn't received the details of her alias yet. "Sort of all over," she hedged.

"Ha! Ask you a question, you tell me a lie. I deserve that for being so nosy, I guess."

Sydney shifted in the couch. It was like quicksand. "No, really, I've sort of grown up all over the country."

"You have no accent! You sound so educated, so refined. I knew you didn't belong in this building the moment I saw you walk in. But there's no shame in hiding. I've been hiding for ten years, since Samson was taken."

There was something about the way she said this that caught Sydney off guard. "Taken?" she asked. She half expected her neighbor to tell her Samson had been abducted by aliens and probed to death.

But Mrs. Andropov set her plate down. "In Chechnya. It was the Spetsnaz," she whispered.

Spetsnaz were the elite special forces of the Russian military, the equivalent of the navy's SEALs or the army's Green Berets. They were renowned for their stealth and feared for their brutality.

Mrs. Andropov stabbed her fork into her food, taking her repressed aggression out on the vareniki. "We were taking the bus to work when they stopped us. They informed us a Chechen rebel was on the bus with us and we weren't going anywhere. My Samson smiled and said, 'Can I tell my boss I'll be late?'" She turned to address the ceiling. "You always had to make jokes at the wrong time, didn't you?" She shook her head, still disappointed in him.

"I still remember the way they laughed after they shot him," Mrs. Andropov said. "And their rings. They way they glinted in the sunlight. Trust me," Mrs.

Andropov said, waggling her fork at Sydney. "You find the ones you love, you don't let go. You only have so many years to spend together. And you have the rest of your life to be alone."

* * *

The bar was a hole-in-the-wall place called the Screaming Boar. Sydney missed it the first two times she circled the block on the edge of the Moscow State University campus, until she noticed a wooden sign with an animal that looked vaguely boarlike. The animal had several spears sticking out of it and seemed to be letting loose a strange death cry. The grotesque picture notwithstanding, the bar itself was rather cozy. A thick coating of dust had settled on the bar, the booths, and the bottles, giving the place a hazy glow. And it had the pleasant, quiet vibe of a local pub.

Sydney recognized the hunched-over man wearing a cheap tweed coat in one of the booths. He held a glass of dark liquor to his lips, his mouth stuck in a perpetual scowl. The downturned lines only accented the deep wrinkles in his face, which the picture she was shown at SD-6 hadn't done justice.

She slipped into his booth. "Central Park is beautiful in the summer," she said.

The man stared at her with dead eyes. "Why don't

you just stand up and *announce* that you're a spy?" he snorted.

Sydney froze. "I'm sorry. I thought you were someone else."

"No, no, no. I'm supposed to say, 'Yet it is much more humid than our beloved Russia,' and you say, 'The dry heat is overrated.' And we go on pretending we make a difference in this world."

Sydney stared at him, stunned. "You're Anatoly Gromnovich?"

"In the flesh," he muttered, signaling for another drink.

Sydney had read about his type. Gromnovich was one of Those Spies.

In her line of work, operatives inevitably went through a bell curve of experience. They started with limitless excitement for their job, and after their first few missions they were on a high they thought they'd never lose. But as they progressed, the endless double crosses and shifting allegiances wore them out. Very few survived past fifty without descending on the other side of the bell curve as one of Them.

The old. The tired. The depressed. The alcoholics.

Sydney had adopted her own level of distrust—it was a must for her personal safety. She never doubted the validity of her cause. And she was lucky that she worked for an organization she knew was doing the right thing. But when she looked in Gromnovich's eyes, she saw a man who'd been betrayed enough times that he didn't care anymore. A man who didn't need to follow protocol when it came to exchanging code words because, *pffffft,* what does it matter? We'll all be dead in a couple years.

Throw in a couple hand waves ("Bah!"), heat at a degree warm enough to melt the Cold War so that these men feel even more dispossessed, and let simmer for four years. Voilà. The recipe for Grumpy Old Spy was complete.

"Do you have the dossier?" she asked. The best way to deal with Them was to keep conversation to a minimum.

He pulled one out of a leather satchel. "Congratulations," he said. "You've just finished two years of classes at the Maskyutov Complex in the Ural Mountains and successfully transferred to the Moscow State University."

Inside the dossier was a driver's license and passport. Her transcripts from the college in the Urals showed solid but not distinguished grades with an emphasis on technical classes in audiovisual systems.

"What's the significance of my course load?" she asked. "It doesn't make sense that I'm still undeclared after my second year."

"Remaining undeclared makes you appear wishy-washy, thus, easy for K-Directorate to manipulate. Also," he said with a smile, "I didn't want to build an identity that was too tough for you remember."

Her cheeks flushed. It was typical condescension from one of Them.

Sydney grabbed the dossier. "Thanks."

"How old are you?" he asked quietly.

She hesitated. "Nineteen."

"I have bunions older than you. How many missions have you been on? Six?"

"Eight."

"Perfect. How many men have you killed?"

"I'm not going to have this conversation."

"No, no," he reached for her, at once serious and apologetic. "Please. For an old man's edification. Tell me this, at least: the men you killed—did they deserve it?"

"I don't think of it in those terms."

"A novice's answer."

He was drawing her in, sharpening his claws. But she couldn't stop herself. "Why does that make me a novice? Because I haven't . . ." She lowered her voice and leaned in. "Because I haven't killed as many people as you have?"

"No," he countered. "That makes you naïve. And I weep at the idea of what you're going to find out when you have to kill someone you don't know, or worse, one of your own. You don't know even know about *Sloane*—"

He stopped himself as the bartender arrived with his drink.

"What about Sloane?" Sydney asked icily.

"Nothing," Gromnovich replied, in control of his temper again. "But there's a difference between being naïve and being a novice. What makes you fall into both categories is that you're ready to walk out of here without learning how you're going to meet our SD-9 mole."

The worst part about Them? Sometimes They were right.

"It's very simple," he said after Sydney set the dossier back on the table. "Come back here tonight, sit in this booth. Our man will find you and initiate contact."

"Got it."

"We're not done."

Sydney felt the air of a sharp reply fill her lungs. But she held it in.

"If you get into real trouble and need to be extracted, come back here. Sit in this booth and order the twelve-year-old scotch." He held up his drink as Exhibit A. "Then go to the women's bathroom and wait. We'll get the signal."

Sydney waited while Gromnovich took his sweet time finishing the drink.

"Are we done?"

"Yes. Now we're done."

Sydney was standing to leave when she heard him say, in English, "Oh, and Miss Bristow?" A chill ran down her spine at the mention of her name. She looked at him.

He toasted her with a sneer. "Good luck."

5

MY NAME IS SASHA Petrova.

My birthday is March 19, 1974.

I was born in the town of Ekaterinburg, in the Ural Mountains.

My mother died in a car accident when I was seven. My father is still alive, but I don't talk to him much.

Even though Gromnovich was a pain in the butt, Sydney had to admit that using true personal details as parts of her alias made things easier to remember.

"Incoming!"

Sydney ducked her head closer to the copy of *Pravda* she wasn't reading. A beer stein smashed into the wall above her, and though no shards of glass rained down on her this time, she did feel the now-familiar residual spray of beer.

The Screaming Boar at night was a very different place than during the day.

She had posted herself at the designated booth promptly at 7:30, regulating her consumption to water, soda, and, when she was ready for the hard stuff, coffee. For three hours, she'd fended off the advances of increasingly pushy men who couldn't understand why an attractive coed didn't want to talk to them. The happy-hour yokels gave way to the tired businessmen, who in turn ceded ground to the rowdy college crowd. And the recently graduated seniors were by far the worst.

"Coffee?" one of them bellowed when Sydney placed her order. "We don't drink coffee here. Let me buy you something that will put hair on your chest." Sydney demurred, opting to take what little time she had left to go over the details of the alias Gromnovich had set up for her.

My name is Sasha Petrova.

I would like to pursue a career in video support for a private security firm.

No, I haven't declared a major yet. But I have a passion for English literature. I guess because my mother was a teacher.

She saw him approaching out of the corner of her eye. It was Mr. Coffee, this time backed up by a group of his friends. He put a drink down in front of her and helped himself to her booth. His friends piled in after him.

"Come around yet?" he asked.

This was the last thing she needed, a bunch of drunks intruding on her mission. "Thanks, guys, really. I'm waiting for somebody."

The seniors let out a collective laugh. It wasn't sustained. It was more like one group "Ha."

Mr. Coffee leaned in closer. He reeked of beer and cigarettes, a combination that reminded her of rescuing Francie from one too many frat house basements. Drunk Russian college oafs were no better than American ones, apparently.

"Then where is he?" he asked. "I see a beautiful girl like you, sitting by her lonesome . . ." He trailed off, losing his train of thought. " 'S a crime, is what it is," he rallied.

Sydney smiled politely. But she had to end this now.

"You know, where I come from," she told him, steel beneath her smile, "when a woman shoots you down, the polite thing to do is move on."

Another group "Ha," but this one was uncertain,

as if the guys had taken the single syllable and turned it into two. Like "Haaaa-wha?" Mr. Coffee's attitude shifted instantly.

"Who do you think you are?" he asked in an angry whisper.

"She's trying to let you escape with some semblance of dignity."

All heads in the booth turned. Standing at the table was an elegantly dressed woman in her late twenties. "The young girl asked you nicely to leave," the woman said. "Now I'm ordering you."

It was a voice of maturity, authority. The way she said it, Sydney immediately had to rethink her conceptions about the SD-9 mole.

She'd assumed it would be a man. She was wrong.

There was something about seeing an older woman humiliate younger guys. No matter how smooth or smart, they simply had no decent comeback. All Mr. Coffee could muster was a defiant glare, until he mumbled, "C'mon, guys, let's find some real women worth talking to."

They shuffled out of the booth. "Try not to trip on your bruised ego on your way out," the woman muttered. Mr. Coffee turned, furious, but said nothing.

The woman sat down. "You looked like you needed some help."

"Yeah, I guess you could say that."

"My name is Diana Ivanov."

"Sasha Petrova."

"Are you really waiting for somebody, or did you just want those lovely gentlemen to leave you alone?"

Sydney felt a vibration on the table.

"Actually, I was—" Sydney stopped. The vibration had a pattern.

Dot-dot-dash-dot-dot.

It was Morse code.

Diana was tapping out a message on the underside of the table, measured out not by the length of taps but the length of silence between them. Sydney let her hands rest on top of the table, reading what this charming, attractive mole was trying to tell her.

S-T-I-L-L—U-N-D-E-R—

"I was just . . . trying to enjoy a cup of coffee," Sydney replied slowly.

S-U-R-V-E-I-L-L-A-N-C-E—D-O—N-O-T—

"You could have found a better coffee shop, that's for sure." Diana laughed.

—B-R-E-A-K—C-O-V-E-R—F-O-L-L-O-W— M-E—

"Tell me," Diana said, "would you mind accompanying me? I have an interesting opportunity to explain to you."

O-U-T—O-F—T-H-E—B-A-R—

"Naturally, you don't have to. We just met, after all—"

"Let's go," Sydney interrupted.

Sydney felt someone staring at them as they left. It was Mr. Coffee and his crew. He stood and gestured for his buddies to follow as Sydney reached the door with Diana. "I think we have a problem," she whispered.

Diana stopped, turned, and flashed a wicked grin at Sydney's would-be boyfriend. "Or an opportunity."

The night air was cool and clean compared to the staleness in the bar. Diana moved quickly down the street, and Sydney had to break into a trot to keep up with her new handler's fast pace.

"Sasha, are you familiar with the SVR?"

"Yeah, it's like the KGB, right?" The playacting felt ridiculous, but they didn't have a choice. K-Directorate was still listening in.

Diana paused at the entrance to an alley behind the bar. She looked over Sydney's shoulder, making sure the men from the bar saw where they were.

"I work for a branch of the new KGB called K-Directorate," Diana explained absentmindedly. "And we've been watching you for a while." She turned back to Sydney and rolled her eyes. "Of course, it's all different now. We're completely legitimate. We don't snoop into anyone's private life. But we'd like you to consider joining."

It was surreal. Diana was using the same language Sydney heard when she joined the CIA. Except K-Directorate was a false front, a pretend black ops arm for the KGB that was only interested in consolidating its own power. SD-6 was *real*.

When the men were within twenty-five feet, Diana pulled Sydney into the alley. They hadn't gone very far before reaching a dead end. "What are you *doing*?" Sydney whispered.

Diana reached into her jacket pocket and pulled out a pair of brass knuckles. "We need a distraction," she whispered back. "Hope you're as good as they say you are."

Sydney turned to see that Mr. Coffee and his gang had cut off their only way out. "Well, well, well," Mr. Coffee said with a chuckle. "What was that you were saying about my *dignity*?"

"It's about to get a lot worse" was all Sydney could come up with. Diana glanced at her. Sydney shrugged. Trash talking wasn't her strength.

"You," Mr. Coffee sputtered. "You're *dead*."

He flew at Sydney, but she was ready for him. She sidestepped at the last second and sent him flying into the heap of trash that had overflowed the Dumpster outside the bar. Another goon was right behind him, but Sydney made a three-quarter turn, lashing her leg out and catching him in the sternum. He crumpled, down for the count.

Sydney turned to see that Diana was handling herself capably. She already had one of the other two remaining goons in a headlock, rabbit-punching him with her free hand. But her free hand was the one with the brass knuckles. So every punch broke the goon's nose a little more.

The remaining friend of Mr. Coffee hesitated, confused. This wasn't how back alley brawls were supposed to go, especially against two women. Deciding he was outmatched, he ran.

A sedan screeched out of nowhere and cut off his escape. Two plainclothes agents stepped out of the car and screamed, "Hands in the air!" The car was unmarked, but the agents were as well-dressed as Diana.

They weren't cops. They were K-Directorate.

A yell emerged from behind her. Sydney spun to see Mr. Coffee giving it one last go. She dodged right, which he expected, then cut back left, which he didn't. He threw out his arm in a wide arc, trying for her hair. She looped her arm around his and used his centrifugal force to spin him against the brick wall.

With one punch, she smashed his voice box. His hands flew up to his throat and he made a mewling sound.

"Diana, you okay?" one of the agents asked.

"Yeah, we're fine." Diana grabbed Sydney and escorted her out of the alley, leaving Mr. Coffee behind to sink to his knees, convinced he was choking to death.

"New blood can handle herself," the other plainclothes said appreciatively.

Wait, Sydney thought, *they're talking about me.*

"Yeah," Diana said, patting Sydney on the back. "Told you she'd be a worthwhile pickup. Can you clean this?"

"Sure," the first agent said. "We'll call in another unit to shadow you."

Diana picked up her pace and led Sydney to a subway entrance. "Hurry," she murmured, "before they notice we're gone."

* * *

Diana Ivanov wasn't her real name.

She wouldn't tell Sydney who she really was, nor did she have any interest in Sydney's personal history. "It's easier that way," she said when they got back to Sydney's apartment.

When Sydney pushed, Diana admitted that she had gotten her start as an antigovernment rebel in Romania during the last days of the Ceausescu regime. "It was a massacre," Diana said, emotionless. "He kept trying to kill us as fast as he could, to stamp us out as if he could stop the flow of history. They had me, too. The secret police. I was tried and set to be executed the following morning."

"How'd you get out of it?"

Diana sighed, annoyed Sydney was making her reveal this much. "A man bought my freedom."

"Bought it?"

"Yes. And in exchange, he made me work for SD-9."

"Didn't that make you mad?"

"No."

"Why not?"

"Because he taught me both manners and how to shoot a gun. Even if I somehow hadn't been held in prison, I wouldn't have lasted another month on the streets. It was because of him that K-Directorate accepted me as one of their own. Can we talk about something else, please?"

Sydney studied Diana, fascinated. By Sydney's calculations, Diana had been doing this for maybe ten years. But she carried herself with a detached air, as if being a spy were almost an afterthought. There was a sadness, too, especially in her reluctance to share personal information. Personal ties could be used against you. Better not to form any; that way you could never be compromised, never be disappointed.

How many friends has she lost? Sydney wondered. *How many loved ones?*

"K-Directorate," Diana said, interrupting Sydney's thoughts, "had their roots in Chernobyl."

Of course, Sydney knew about the near-meltdown at a nuclear reactor in the Ukraine in 1986. It had been declared a result of human error and poor design.

But if Sydney understood what Diana was saying, the disaster had been no accident. K-Directorate had planned it.

"Wait," Sydney said. "Back up. How is that possible?"

"They made sure they could salvage the operation if it reached crisis proportions—killing millions, polluting the Moscow water supply. Which it never did."

Sydney couldn't wrap her head around what she was hearing. It was too big. "They could have killed *billions* of people," she said.

"Could've. But they didn't I've seen the documents," Diana said. "K-Directorate had a fifteen-year plan to remove the last vestiges of the old ruling elite from power and wipe the slate clean. They hoped the power vacuum would give way to a revolution that would put an oligarchy in place. Maybe there would be elections every few years, to give the people the illusion they were living in a democracy and making a difference. But those in control would be K-Directorate puppets."

"That's why SD-6 needs us to download the virus," Sydney said, understanding the full ramifications of her mission for the first time.

"Not just SD-6. All of the SD cells. The X-ray that the virus will give us inside K-Directorate is the only hope we have of stopping them. And if SD-9 wants to survive, we need that intel. Fast."

SD-9 was the newest SD branch—and the weakest, because of the K-Directorate behemoth that swatted it down as if it were an annoying fly.

"They told you about how deep K-Directorate would go into your background?" Diana asked her.

"Yes."

"Good." Studying Sydney, she added, "Cut your hair."

"Why?"

Diana opened the door to the flat. Instead of saying good-bye, she said, "Because you've come up against K-Directorate agents before. The last thing we need is somebody recognizing you." With that, she was gone.

Sydney thought about Diana's coldness and Gromnovich's disgust. *Maybe to be a good spy, or maybe just to survive, you have to give up depending on anybody.*

But another part of her said, *God, I hope that's not true.*

6

AS SYDNEY CROSSED INTO the technical district of the city, she could still smell her singed hair.

Not prepared to cut it, she had borrowed Mrs. Andropov's curling iron the night before, and when her neighbor saw the results, she had shrieked, "Strange girl, what have you done?"

Next time, Sydney thought, *bring a wig.*

She entered the empty lobby of Comcor Industries. "Can I help you?" asked the receptionist.

"Sasha Petrova," Sydney replied, smoothing her plain black skirt. "I have a nine a.m. appointment with Mr. Ulee."

The receptionist looked down at her schedule. "We don't have you down." She frowned. "Wait a second." Her hand drifted below the desk.

Out of nowhere, three armed guards entered the lobby, pointing AR-15s at Sydney, who raised her hands in shock. The receptionist was still looking over the schedule, frowning.

"You've taken a wrong turn," one of the guards said. "Turn around."

Sydney froze. Diana hadn't told her about this.

"You have seven seconds to realize your mistake and correct it," the second guard said. "We advise you do that by walking in the opposite direction."

"Diana Ivanov told me to report here," Sydney announced, trying to keep her voice calm.

"Miss, this is your last warning," the third guard said.

"Oh, wait," the receptionist chimed in, holding up the schedule. "Here she is."

The guards lowered their weapons. "Sorry," the first one said. "Protocol."

"Do you ever shoot people by mistake?" Sydney asked, trying to smile.

"All the time."

"Follow the white line," the third one said.

What white line? Sydney wondered. But when she looked up, she saw that a small door next to the elevators had swung open. She hadn't noticed it before—it blended in perfectly with its surroundings. But now it beckoned her with the promise of a white line and a dark hallway.

When Sydney poked her head in, she saw that the path was illuminated by a bare hundred-watt bulb about fifty feet in the distance. She approached the bulb, expecting another door. Instead, the hallway continued. Sydney kept walking, now venturing into inky darkness. The light behind her clicked off. But before she could trip over her own feet, another light yet another fifty feet ahead of her turned on, guiding her way. This continued for six lights, completely throwing off Sydney's sense of direction.

Finally, she reached an elevator. The doors were open, waiting for her. The moment she stepped in, the doors closed and the elevator descended. Unlike the SD-6 elevator, this one had no buttons or numbers.

When the doors opened, Diana was waiting for her. "Welcome," she said, "to K-Directorate."

As Diana led her into a gigantic bullpen that comprised the east wing of the complex, Sydney glanced around. The operations center was a converted military base, abandoned by the government fifteen years ago, according to her handler. It had been built as a base the Kremlin could scramble to in case of emergency or attack. But when Moscow couldn't pay to keep the lights on anymore, K-Directorate had bought it. The offices boasted the most cutting-edge technology available, but it was impossible to avoid a military vibe, in comparison to the sleek corporate atmosphere of SD-6.

K-Directorate was also cold. *Cold enough to see my breath,* Sydney thought, exhaling. She shivered as she followed Diana down the halls.

Diana stopped at a small kitchen jutting off from the east wing. "Orientation starts in an hour," Diana said. "We'll make sure you get a good seat. Just remember—"

Another woman entered the kitchen, cutting off Diana's last piece of advice. Her mouth turned up in a half smile. "Diana, is this your new recruit?"

"Sasha Petrova," Diana said, stepping back as Sydney smiled brightly, "meet Anna Espinosa."

Anna had long, thick dark hair pulled back in a clip, and penetrating brown eyes. She wore black fatigues. Around her hips was a low-slung black leather belt containing a holstered pistol.

"Are you going to join our recon unit?" Anna asked, studying her.

"Uh, we'll see," Sydney replied. "Have to crawl before I can walk."

"We'll probably start her in video tech support," Diana added.

"Oh, that reminds me," Anna said, frowning slightly. "I have to go make an example out of some techie who left us high and dry."

"Anna, wait—" The blood drained from Diana's face.

"Nice to meet you," Anna said to Sydney as she turned on her heavy boots and walked away.

"Is she Cuban?" Sydney asked. "I thought I heard a trace of—"

"Shhhh." Diana held up a finger, paused at the kitchen door, and watched intently.

Anna marched to the middle of the wing.

"Ladies and gentlemen," she called out. "May I have your attention, please?"

Three troopers, dressed in identical paramilitary garb, materialized at different points in the wing. They watched Anna closely. One of them had a smile on his face.

The office fell silent, rapt with fear, as Anna announced, "Would Aleksander Vladinov please rise?"

A cowering man of about thirty stood up, trembling. His white shirt stuck to him with a thin glaze of perspiration. "Aleksander," Anna explained, "left his Recon Unit stranded in an eight-story apartment building with no fire escapes and no working elevators."

Sydney's pulse sped up as she watched Aleksander look around.

"It's not my fault," he said nervously. "The electronic blueprints K-Directorate gave me indicated—"

Anna calmly unholstered her pistol. Sydney gasped. She wasn't the only one.

"He's beyond saving," Diana whispered over her shoulder. What she really meant was, *There's nothing we can do. So don't intervene.*

Anna didn't point her 9mm Beretta at Aleksander. She didn't have to. The threat was enough. She turned in a slow circle, addressing the entire wing. "When one of you fails," she shouted, "all of you fail! As a result, we need to review the basics of video tech support."

Aleksander suddenly broke down into tears. He remained standing, but his sobs were long and wailing, and all he could do to hide the shame was cover his face with his hands.

Sydney stood motionless, feeling sick. She wanted to do something, but what? Aleksander probably wouldn't be walking away from this alive. And he knew it.

She could tell by the faces of the other office workers that they'd seen this before. Anna's lesson was nothing new to them.

"What's the first thing they teach you in video tech support?" Anna asked.

"It's never the system's fault," everyone in the office except Sydney answered, their voices blending.

"What's the single greatest source of error in video surveillance?"

"Human error," everyone in the office said back.

"Aleksander," Anna said, turning back to her prey. "I'll pose the question. Whose fault was it that we were left scrambling for an escape route?"

"My fault," he sniffled. "It was my fault."

Anna holstered her weapon. "Good," she said. "Very good." Aleksander, along with the rest of the office, let out a sigh of relief.

Anna turned to her partners, who still watched, amused, from the corners. "Take him down to human resources."

"No!" Aleksander screamed. Two of the paratroopers marched forward and grabbed him by an arm. They dragged him away from his terminal as he begged, "Please—not human resources! *Please!*" They reached the elevator that presumably led farther down into the pits of K-Directorate. "I'm *sorry*!" was all Aleksander had time to shriek before the doors closed on him.

Sydney shut her eyes, fighting the urge to clamp her hands over her ears. When she opened them, she was astonished to see Anna walking away, whistling, as if nothing had happened. Anna caught sight of Sydney and Diana framed in the doorway and flipped them a jaunty salute. *Welcome aboard! Be seein' ya! Try not to screw up or else you'll be the next one I send to human resources!*

She was a bully, that was obvious. What made her dangerous was that she believed in her cause. She was the kind who said, *Hey, sometimes you gotta kick a little butt to make your point.* She was the stereotypical marine drill instructor. She was the trigonometry teacher who had shaken his head when Sydney was at the board and said, "Bristow, you just don't *get* it, do you?"

Yes, Sydney knew the type. And she knew the best thing she could do was stay out of Anna's way.

Diana's cell phone rang, seeming abnormally loud in the silence following Anna's demonstration. "Yes?" Diana answered. Her eyes flicked up to Sydney. "Yes, I'll send her right in."

Diana hung up. "What is it?" Sydney asked.

"My boss wants to meet you."

* * *

Throughout her life, Sydney had had a healthy distrust of hypnotism.

She believed it could work on weak-minded people, of course. People who were easily persuaded, people who were distracted or unaware of subtle manipulation and cues the hypnotist was giving out. And she'd read the SD-6 psych ops reports detailing methods of mind control. A strobe light, at the right frequency and wattage, could induce sleep. Certain drug regimens made targets more docile and open to suggestion.

But the idea that someone could look into Sydney's eyes and say, "By the count of three, you'll be under my spell," had always been vaguely laughable to her. It would take more than a soothing voice and a timepiece swinging back and forth to make her cluck like a chicken or forget her best friend's name.

But when the director of operations at K-Directorate rose from behind the giant desk in his office, walked around it, and shook Sydney's hand, she had to rethink her position on the matter.

His name was Pietr Gregoran.

He was very happy to have her on his team.

Would she like to have a seat?

These words registered somewhere in the back of Sydney's head, but she didn't really comprehend them. She also didn't remember her brain giving her mouth the signal to say:

"Oh, hello."

"Thank you. It's good to be here."

"I'd love to sit."

It didn't hurt that he was stunningly handsome.

Just over six feet tall, he carried himself with the swagger of a man who didn't need to be told how attractive he was. His teeth, his hair, his clothes, all were perfect.

His youth also made an impact on Sydney. This man, who held roughly the same position as Arvin Sloane, had to be between thirty and thirty-five years old. *How is that possible?* she thought. *If K-Directorate is as powerful as Diana said, how could he ascend that rapidly?*

But what really shook Sydney were his eyes. They were dark green, like a lush forest, with tiny flecks in the iris. They were so captivating, she could study them for hours—Wait, what did he just ask her?

"I said tell me about yourself."

Oh, okay. My name is Sydney Bristow, I'm here as a double agent from SD-6 to expose your intelligence organization, and I like dogs and Scrabble. Do you like Italian food?

"If this is K-Directorate, shouldn't you already know everything?" she asked with a smile. She was trying to break the mood and snap out of this strange trance his eyes had drawn her into.

"We do," Gregoran answered. "But I'd like to hear your version."

He made this seem charming and harmless. But it

wasn't. He was testing her, probing her for weakness. Sloane's words came back to her.

They will test you. They will lie to you. They'll try to get you to contradict yourself, and you won't even notice.

And despite the way he captivated her, she forced herself to concentrate on every word coming from his mouth.

"Where are you from?"

"The Urals."

"What are you doing here?"

"Attending summer session at Moscow State University. I was just looking for a way to make some money, I never thought I'd end up working for the KGB." Another smile. It had no effect.

"Are you parents still in the Urals?"

"My mother passed away. But my father's still there. We're not very close."

"He has cancer."

A statement. Not a question. *He has cancer.* It was a minor point that Gromnovich had thrown into the dossier. The reason was simple. If somebody investigated too closely, Sasha Petrova's father would die after a long illness. Gromnovich hadn't included any backup information on the cancer. Yet Gregoran had immediately sought some out, a sixth sense, perhaps, that told him she was weak on this subject.

"Yes," Sydney replied.

"What kind?"

She had to make something up. "Lung."

"That's a shame."

"The carcinogens from the mines seeped into our water," Sydney said, warming up to the lie. "There's been a dramatic increase in the incidence of cancer there."

"Yes," Gregoran replied. "But that was leukemia. Not lung cancer."

Sydney paused for half a second. "Cancer is cancer. Who can predict such things?"

"Very true. Did you boil your water?"

This was a reference to an old wives' tale in the Urals. The idea was that if you boiled your water, you would kill the cancer-causing chemicals. It didn't work, but the locals clung to it, needing to believe there was a way to avert this terrifying plague.

What he really wanted to know was *How gullible are you?*

"Every day," Sydney said.

"We clean our water," Gregoran sighed. "We clean our lives. But we don't clean what's important." It was a strange digression, almost as if Gregoran were trying to build a philosophical bridge to her. *I know what you've gone through,* his eyes said. *Your government has failed you, but K-Directorate won't.*

But that's not what stopped Sydney. What stopped her was the *way* he said it.

We clean our water. . . . We clean our lives. . . .

She had heard it before.

"Any siblings?" he asked.

"An older brother. He died in Afghanistan. I . . . was very little."

We clean our water. . . . We clean our lives . . . but we don't clean what's important. . . .

It was something she'd read.

She remembered that now.

A transcript at SD-6. Some sort of . . . was it a rally?

Think! she prodded herself. *I know this man somehow! I've heard him, I've read about him, I've—*

"What else?"

"Excuse me?"

"What else can you tell me?"

"That's really about it," Sydney said. "Not much of a life, I guess."

"I don't believe you. When somebody can summarize her life in five minutes, they're fooling themselves."

And suddenly, Sydney placed him.

His name, ten years before, was Josef.

Sydney had researched him as part of an intelligence brief on international cult leaders that she'd written for SD-6 before she was cleared for missions. As charismatic figures went, Josef was strictly third-string. He traveled the Russian countryside, setting himself up as the messiah of the Soviet Union, promising poor farmers that he could succeed where the state had failed. He'd become a fugitive from the Kremlin, which had only increased the power of his legend.

But what had made him unique among demagogues, Sydney remembered, was his success in eluding any kind of photography during his barn-burning revivals. Most power seekers were obsessed about broadcasting their picture on as many media outlets as possible. But Josef, who had known he was being hunted by the KGB, had dodged attempts to take his picture. Since most of Josef's faithful couldn't afford a camera anyway, this rarely had presented a problem.

But at one of his gatherings, somebody had snuck in a tape recording. Frustrated in their attempts to hunt for "a beautiful twenty-year-old boy with gorgeous green eyes" (as all witness statements read), the KGB had analyzed the tape in minute detail. When Sydney had heard it, she hadn't been able to understand why so many people would follow Josef to the point of financial ruin, though his preacher's cadence and his repetition of phrases might make him an easy sell to the uneducated masses.

Now, as she sat in front of him, staring into his eyes, being absorbed into his presence, it all made perfect sense.

Of course, she might be mistaken. With only a tape recording and eyewitness descriptions to identify Josef, there was no way to confirm that Gregoran was the same man.

Actually, there was one way.

Sydney remembered that one of Josef's habits was to end all of his sermons the same way: with a chant. As the collection plate was passed around, he would lead his flock to repeat over and over, "We put our faith in the land and our faith in God." It would start quietly. Then Josef would make it build until it shook the rafters. The gatherings would end when he shouted back, "And I put my faith in you!"

Gregoran smiled and stood from the desk. "Well, when you feel comfortable telling me more, I look forward to getting to know you."

She needed something. Something to prove her suspicions.

"I'm just an old-fashioned girl," she said with a shrug. "I was always taught to put my faith in God and in the land."

"And I," Gregoran said, "find that charming."

7

THE REST OF SYDNEY'S day at K-Directorate was taken up by orientation. Sydney sat through a boring training session on how to navigate the company's extensive surveillance network. She mastered it in five minutes and spent the rest of the day thinking about Gregoran.

I said too much, she thought. *Now he knows I'm on to him.*

Diana called her on her SD-6 cell the moment she got home from work to set up a debrief. Sydney quickly outlined her encounter in the director's office, as well as her suspicions. Diana fell silent, then said, "Meet me at the following location. I'll find out what I can. The location was a bank of satellites on the edge of the city, where television signals were broadcast. The electromagnetic frequencies would prevent any K-Directorate microphones from picking them up.

Diana was already waiting for her when she arrived. "What did you find out?" Sydney asked anxiously.

"Nothing. If Gregoran has a secret past, he's ensured it's going to stay hidden."

"We can use this, can't we?" Sydney asked. "A guy like Gregoran doesn't make director without stepping on the backs of a lot of people. Somebody *has* to be interested in finding out the truth."

"Unless K-Directorate hired him for exactly that reason," Diana countered. "Who better to lead a mass delusion that we're all working for the KGB than a zealot?"

Sydney had considered this. "I'm not talking about upper management. I'm talking about the KGB grunts who combed the countryside hunting for Josef. Some of them have still got to be ticked off they didn't find him, and they'll be even *more* ticked off to learn they're working side by side with him."

Diana closed her eyes tightly, as if concentrating on a math problem. "We have a strategic advantage," she agreed. "We just have to figure out how to use it."

"No, you *had* a strategic advantage." Sydney had heard that gruff voice before. Her heart sank as Anatoly Gromnovich emerged from the shadows. "But you squandered it the moment you dropped bait for him."

"What's he doing here?" Sydney demanded.

"My options for snooping into Gregoran's past are limited," Diana replied. "Gromnovich was my handler. There's nobody better for this kind of work."

Sydney turned from Diana to Gromnovich, then back to Diana. "*He's* your handler? He's the one you told me about?"

"Surprise," Gromnovich said, lighting a cigarette. "Needless to say, I'd be able to do my job a lot better if you hadn't overplayed your hand."

"I needed confirmation," Sydney said defensively.

"And did you get it?" Gromnovich fired back. "No. Worst-case scenario, this is a wild-goose chase. Based on what? Your gut? Best-case scenario, this man is the cornfield Jesus you say he is. Except he's aware that we're investigating him. Either way, we are—as you Americans say, poop out of luck."

It was as if Gromnovich had opened up her brain,

peered inside, and pulled out her biggest insecurity. He confirmed what she had been most worried about: she had gone a step too far.

"What did the two of you talk about?" Diana asked.

"Where I was from. My family."

"Was he direct? Did he cut you off?"

"No," Sydney said. "He was actually pretty pleasant. Like he wanted to be my friend."

A silent look passed between Diana and Gromnovich. "She's not good enough," Gromnovich said under his breath.

"What?" Sydney asked.

"I don't think we have a choice," Diana said back to him.

"What?" Sydney insisted.

Diana turned to her. "Gregoran considers himself a ladies' man. It's likely you're the next object of his affections."

Sydney blushed. "He's fifteen years older than me."

"Precisely," Gromnovich replied.

"He called me and had me send you into his office," Diana said. "Alone. He must have seen you on one of the internal feeds and was taken by you."

"And his seemingly innocent questions?" Gromnovich added. "He was looking for ammunition.

Surely you've had such conversations before." Gromnovich mimed a slouched-over American college student. "'So, what's your major? Uh-huh . . . That's fascinating.' All a pretext to get you into bed."

Sydney stared, open-mouthed. She *had* had a conversation like that. With Noah.

The night in Griffith Park

Was he really interested in who she was? Or was it just . . . ammunition?

"I'll do what I can," Gromnovich said. "But if Diana is right, you're in a better position than any of us to find out about Gregoran's past. It's perfect pillow talk, especially if he believes you were a former disciple."

"I am not sleeping with him," Sydney said emphatically.

"Even better," Gromnovich answered. "A man of his ego, it's not about sex. It's about seduction and power. Adore him. Worship him. But the more he attempts to woo you, the more you resist. And the more it will drive him insane."

Diana read the confusion on Sydney's face. "You've played hard to get, haven't you? It's no different."

But she hadn't. At least, not on purpose.

She'd pushed Burke away because she couldn't

fit him into her life, not with college and SD-6 intervening.

And Noah? He'd been playing hard to get since they'd started dating.

"I—I guess," she said after a pause.

"For God's sake," Gromnovich cried out in exasperation as Sydney fell silent. "Do I have take you shopping for a training bra after this?"

"Anatoly!" Diana barked. But Gromnovich threw up his hands.

"I'll take care of this," Diana said, leading Sydney away.

"What are you going to do?" Gromnovich called after them. "Explain to her the birds and the bees?"

"I'm going to teach her what you never taught me. What I had to learn for myself."

Gromnovich snorted. "What's that?"

"That women make better spies than men."

*　*　*

Dancing in college—anywhere in Los Angeles, really—was like being thrown into the deep end of a pool. At frat parties and nightclubs all over Westwood, Sydney would find herself surrounded by people who could *move*. They effortlessly found the beat in a way that was foreign to her. And while she could keep time, she couldn't compete with the lithe bodies around her. So she inevitably found herself standing against the wall, waving at Francie, who would try to lure her onto the dance floor. The few times Sydney hadn't been able to fight off some guy's advances and had gotten dragged into a throng of people, she'd dreaded the inevitable moment when their eyes would meet and he'd discover she didn't know what to do.

Which is why when Diana asked casually, "What's the one thing that makes you most embarrassed?" Sydney blurted out, "Dancing." She didn't think about it until Diana smiled and said, "Perfect."

She felt the heavy bass before they entered the abandoned warehouse. It took thirty seconds for her eyes to adjust to the darkness inside, but once they did, Sydney had to fight off the need to hyperventilate. The warehouse was crammed with people, all of them dancing. Giant strobe lights cut through a haze of dry ice and cigarette smoke. Wrapped around the upper beams was a gigantic papier-mâché snake that moved its head back and forth over the crowd. In the snake's mouth was a gigantic apple.

"How do you know about this place?" Sydney shouted over the pounding house music.

"K-Directorate monitors the rave scene," Diana

answered. "They're a good petri dish for testing our more addictive drug cocktails." Diana pulled her closer so she could hear over the music. "This is your mission. I want you to make the DJ change his music for you," she said.

Sydney stared at her. "What?"

"Make the DJ change his music."

"How?"

"Well, that's the trick, isn't it? You can't just go up to him and ask. He'll laugh at you. So you have to use *other* means."

Sydney swallowed a lump of nerves and forced it down to her stomach. "This is one of those character-building exercises, isn't it? I'm never good at those."

"Think about your technique," Diana said, ignoring her. "This has to be slow and purposeful. Work it in stages. Start by making him notice you. Then you win him over. Finally, make him work for you."

Sydney nodded, but her mind was going in a million different directions at once. She located the DJ, spinning records on a platform just out of range of the snake's swiveling head. She watched the other dancers, vainly hoping there were some moves she could copy. She tapped her fingers against her legs—not to keep time to the music, but to remind herself that her legs were still there.

"And Sydney? After you make him change his music, I want you to disappear thirty seconds after he's noticed you."

And with that, Diana pushed her on to the dance floor.

It's not that you don't like *dancing,* Sydney told herself, trying to rationalize what she was doing. *It's just that you haven't had much practice.*

The first song must have lasted for more than ten minutes. The relentless *chunk-chunk-chunk-chunk* of the beat exhausted her, but the dancers on all sides of her didn't seem to mind. They threw themselves around exuberantly, arms and legs flailing, but managed never to run into each other. Somehow, every person on the dance floor maintained his or her personal space.

Everyone, that is, except Sydney. She bounced from one foot to the other, trying to feel comfortable. Instead, she stepped on someone's toes and, in the process of apologizing, bumped into someone else.

She glanced up at the DJ. As she watched him, she saw that he actually switched songs often, but they all had the same tempo, making them sound like one endless piece of music. Somewhere, she could hear the familiar guitar chords of Nirvana's "Smells Like Teen Spirit," but sped up almost beyond recognition.

She threw her arms over her head and gently let

her hips rock to the screaming guitar. The song changed to AC/DC's "Back in Black." She smiled at the seamless transition and let herself groove a little more. She bent her knees and slowly rotated, doing her own thing. She let her eyes open slightly, convinced she'd see an audience laughing and pointing at her.

Instead, the floor seemed to open up to accommodate her. She'd carved out her own little space that the rest of the crowd seemed to respect. Emboldened, she let her arms go a little bit, then glanced up at the DJ. To her surprise, he was smiling at her.

Sydney spun away, caught. She forced herself to keep her back to him. For a terrifying five seconds, she thought the self-consciousness would descend again and she'd lose any progress she'd built up over the past . . . five minutes? Ten? Thirty? How long had she been out here, anyway?

The beat didn't change, but the song did. Salt 'N' Pepa's "Push It." Sydney felt a surge of power. The kind she got when she was turning the radio dial and happened upon the perfect song at the perfect moment.

Gradually she slowed down her movements, at once in and out of sync with the music. For the first half of the song, she refused to turn around and acknowledge the DJ. But she could feel the other dancers noticing her—the quick glances from the women and the longer looks from the men. She'd never experienced this before. But the feeling transformed her. She was confident. She let her eyes drift down to the floor . . . then up the wall . . . then to the booth. The DJ was staring at her.

He wasn't smiling anymore. He was enthralled.

Sydney held the gaze, even though she was looking over her shoulder. She slowed her movements down even more. The DJ picked up the message she was sending him. He nodded—partly in time to the music, but partly as if to say to Sydney, *All right, challenge accepted.*

Reaching over, he took the needle on one of the turntables and dragged it across the record with a loud *scraaaaaaaaatch*. The music stopped long enough for the crowd to let out a single "Awwwwwww!"

He started the next song. It was a slow, heavy number. The vocals were impossible to decipher, but they had a dark, threatening sexiness to them. The crowd cheered the change in pace and surged forward in a group slow dance. The pogolike bouncing stopped as the shadowy forms of bodies writhed closer together. The temperature in the club rose.

Sydney glanced back up at the DJ, who was still watching her. As a reward, she flashed him a dazzling smile. The DJ smiled back and began playing the needle over certain grooves, showing off his technique.

That's my cue, Sydney realized. *Exit stage right.*

The tight clutch of the crowd made it easy for her to disappear. Sydney slipped through the club, not stopping to look back. Diana was waiting in front of the wall where Sydney would normally have been standing. She stopped to allow herself one look back. She could see the DJ anxiously scanning the dance floor to see where she'd gone.

"That," Diana said with a satisfied grin, "is how you play hard to get."

Sydney strode out of the club. For the first time since they'd met, she led and Diana followed.

She liked how that felt.

8

THE NEXT DAY, WHEN Sydney reported to work, she was assigned a desk. In one drawer she found a photo of Aleksander, the man Anna had raked over the coals, with his wife and young child. *I guess the cleaning person missed this,* Sydney thought grimly, studying the faces. A part of her hoped that somehow Aleksander had made it home to them the night before. But the other part knew that wasn't possible.

Each video support tech was assigned his or her own cubicle to ensure privacy and keep distraction to a minimum. The last thing techs needed as they sweated out getting a recon unit away from enemy fire was a coworker in his face with mindless office chitchat. The result of privacy, however, was a gloomy silence that descended over the cavernous space, compounded by the freezer-room conditions. SD-6 was certainly no barrel of laughs, and when it was time to work, they worked hard, but they celebrated birthdays, they greeted each other in the halls, they talked about their kids in the kitchen. Even a brief exchange of pleasantries was verboten at K-Directorate.

Except for one person. Her name was Mina.

Mina had approached Sydney during a break in their training the day before. Mina already had a high, squeaky voice, and when she spoke in a whisper, as everyone in K-Directorate was wont to do, she slipped into a register that only dogs could hear.

Their first conversation had been typical enough, with a cursory background check: where Sydney was from, how she had arrived at K-Directorate, and so on. But by the next break, Mina had apparently decided that she was Sydney's new best friend, and it was thus her job to take the new girl under her wing. She gave Sydney her take on how the world worked, specifically how K-Directorate worked. Sydney normally kept a safe distance from such people, but

Mina's blithe amalgamation of misinformation, conspiracy theories, and urban legends made for compelling conversation.

Conversation being a loose term, since Sydney's contributions were limited to "Really?", "Uh-huh," and "You don't say."

"They know where we are at all times," Mina had informed her, offering Sydney half of her sandwich. "They spray us with tiny probes that shoot out through the air vents. But the probes are microscopic, we don't even notice they're there. The only way to kill them is to shave off all your hair and bathe in lye."

"Lye? Really?"

"Oh, yeah. You know what else. I hear they're six years away from a genetic doubling program. On a mysterious island called Cayo Concha. All they need is your DNA and, poof, they can make somebody else look like you."

"Uh-huh."

"And all those guards? Meant to spy on spies? Don't believe it. They're descendants of Nazi storm troopers."

"You don't say."

Thankfully, Mina's cubicle was on the other side of the floor from Sydney's. This morning, as she sneaked into her workspace, trying to avoid being ensnared by her new best friend, Sydney wondered what it was about her that attracted such people. But before she could find a satisfactory answer, her phone lit up.

It was Gregoran. "Could you come into my office, please?"

Flirt, but play hard to get, she told herself as she rose and walked to his office. *He's not going to reveal anything. This time, it's all about piquing his interest. Getting him to notice you.*

She swung the door open, her winningest smile on her face. "Good morn—" she said, and the rest died in her throat.

Anna was already there, sitting on Gregoran's desk, legs crossed, foot bouncing, leaning over to look at something on his computer. Sydney hadn't thought any woman could make black fatigues sexy, but Anna did. Gregoran, her appreciative audience, let his eyes linger on her before even acknowledging that Sydney had entered.

"Sasha," he said, "you know Anna."

"We met yesterday." Sydney swallowed.

"Since Aleksander's removal, Anna's team needs a new video support tech," Gregoran said. "I think you'd be perfect for the job."

The smile Sydney had plastered on her face was stuck there. "Great."

"In fact, she was just detailing for me her next operation."

"We have to go into a building that's off K-Directorate's surveillance grid," Anna explained. "You'll wire in from a remote feed on-site. Meaning you're coming with us on the mission."

"You can handle that, can't you, Petrova?" he asked. "I know you're new, but . . ." And now his gaze lingered on Sydney. "I just have a feeling about you."

Is he flirting? Sydney thought nervously.

Anna noticed too, and a frown flickered over her face as she looked at Sydney. But when Gregoran looked back at her, she was all business again.

"We'll take good care of Petrova, I promise," she said to Gregoran. With a smile so wide Sydney expected to see fangs, Anna added, "It'll be *fun*."

Gregoran focused on Sydney again. "Why don't you go down to munitions and get what you need. Anna will meet you in the garage with the team."

"Great." Had she said anything else since she walked in the room? Somehow, before she'd had the chance to draw him in, she'd ended up being assigned to a mission.

Why pick the new girl, with only one day on the job?

She heard faint murmuring as the door closed behind her. "Do you know what to do?" Gregoran asked.

Anna said something, then chuckled.

And Sydney's blood ran cold.

She was being set up.

Thirty minutes later, it was still the only conclusion Sydney could reach. She sat in the back of a black van, cradling a laptop. Four agents from the recon unit sat on either side of her. Anna sat up front.

Obviously, she had gotten too close to Gregoran's secret. But he couldn't kill her without justification. So he sent her out, untrained, with a team of ruthless killers. When she failed, Anna would be able to send her to human resources and K-Directorate would calmly shred the file they had on Sasha Petrova.

"Sasha," one of the recon agents, a linebacker-sized oaf named Sokolov, asked, "what part of the mountains are you from?"

"I grew up in the countryside, just outside Ufa."

"Where's your accent? I don't hear it." Sokolov casually spun a hunting knife on his palm.

"That's what people said about my mother. . . . I guess I inherited her nonaccent accent." Anna kept staring at her, sizing her up. There was no hint of friendliness on her face.

"You have running water there?" Sokolov probed. "Electricity?" Power shortages were notorious in the Urals.

"We have the occasional brownout," Sydney said.

"Who doesn't?" another agent named Gudenov laughed. "I live in the city and we still get them."

"The only place that doesn't is K-Directorate," the third team member, Boransky, piped up. "And that's because we're on our own grid."

"I want to know more about Petrova," Sokolov murmured. He looked at Anna while he said this, but Anna remained silent, judging. Sydney had a suspicion that Anna had clued Sokolov in to the situation. *After this, we take Petrova to the back of the shed and shoot her.*

Sydney was desperate to change the subject.

"How long have you been a team?" she asked.

"Four years," Boransky replied. "Since Spetsnaz."

Sydney looked around at the agents' hands. With the exception of Gudenov, they were all wearing identical rings.

"You're all former special forces?" she asked.

"We're *still* special forces," Sokolov replied. "You're Spetsnaz until you die."

They leaned forward and bumped fists, the equivalent of a high five. Gudenov, the exception, looked away, embarrassed.

"I was Russian navy," he explained to Sydney. "I'm lucky they even talk to me."

"We still think of you as half a man," Boransky joked. "That's more than Shostoko got."

"Shostoko was also Spetsnaz," Gudenov explained. "But he lost his ring. The only excuse for losing a ring is if they take your hand off with it."

"Or your head," Sokolov smiled.

"Speaking of heads," Boransky added, chuckling, "remember how Shostoko's barely fit in the toilet?"

"Getting it in was fine," Sokolov volleyed. "Getting it out was the problem. The fool honestly thought he was going to drown. I had to tell him, 'Shostoko, if you don't stop struggling, you *will* drown.'"

The chuckles turned into gales of laughter. Sydney tried to smile, like an outsider at a family get-together. She'd seen this behavior before. Trading war stories was a pastime as old as the armed forces themselves. But usually the stories didn't involve torturing your own team members.

"Not in front of her." It was the first thing Anna had said, and the men fell silent.

The van pulled to a stop. The other agents braced themselves. Sydney didn't, and her arm bumped painfully against Sokolov's AR-15.

"Listen up," Anna said. "Since this building isn't on the grid, we have to watch every step. It's a residence hotel. The people who live here are all hiding from somebody. Maybe it's us. Maybe it's the Mafia. Maybe it's those fools at SD-9. Doesn't matter. The last thing we need is to get caught with our pants

down while some addict comes at us with an AK-47."
She turned to Sydney. "That's where you come in."

Boransky pulled up a small panel on the floor of
the van, giving Sydney a direct view to a power-
supply grate they had parked over. Boransky set about
unscrewing the large metal grate as Anna snapped her
fingers in front of Sydney's face. "We need blueprints.
Internal security feed. Whatever they have. Got it?"

"I got it," Sydney replied.

"You sure?" Sokolov asked. "You look like you're
going to throw up. New blood usually does, first time
in the field."

"Just give me the connection," Sydney said, trying to sell the confidence she didn't feel. "I'll take
care of the rest."

You have one secret weapon, Sydney thought, trying to console herself. *Remember, you are a trained
CIA operative!*

Boransky grabbed a long cable. He jammed one
end into an open port leading into the building and
the other end into Sydney's computer. Sydney immediately found a server that housed a security feed. She
poked around on her laptop, found the firewall, and
ran a password-sniffer program.

"Our target's on the ninth floor, in room 9071,"
Anna said to the other team members.

"Hostile?" Gudenov asked.

"Extremely. He's responsible for the compromise of seven of our agents. But this is not a run-and-gun. We're bringing him in for questioning based on his recent activity." She addressed Sokolov specifically. "Don't kill him."

"But we can rough him up a little, right?" Sokolov growled.

Anna turned to Sydney. "Where are we?"

A hazard window popped up on the computer screen. "There's no way around this firewall," Sydney told them. "The best I can do is buy time before the police arrive."

"How much time?"

"Ten minutes," Sydney said. "Maybe less."

Anna glanced at Sokolov, who shrugged. "We've worked under tighter conditions than that," he said.

"Right," Anna said. "Let's do it."

"Give me a minute to loop the feed," Sydney said, crashing through the firewall.

Anna and her men got into position. "Don't leave us out in the cold," she warned. But Sydney ignored this as she accessed the security server. Looping the feed, something she'd been taught the day before, was easy. It was simply a matter of dragging and dropping the camera image on the left to the corresponding one on the right. Since the video quality was a muddy digital feed, the human eye never noticed the small glitch as the loop fed back on itself.

"Go," Sydney said, and the team burst out of the van. Then Gudenov slammed the van door in her face and she had to pick them back up on one of the security feeds. Within five seconds, they'd picked the lock to the delivery entrance and were inside the building.

"Petrova, what do we have?" Anna's voice crackled over her throat-mic headset.

Sydney found the appropriate first-floor camera and located the team's position. "Clear access to the stairwell around the corner," she said. The team moved forward in twos. They stopped at the stairwell. "You're clear up to the second floor," she told them. The team went up the stairs. Even though the whole mission looked and smelled and tasted like a setup, there was a part of Sydney that felt excited about the control she had over them. Right now, at least, their lives were in her hands, not the other way around.

She found the building schematics on the server, opened the document, and navigated her mouse over the blueprints. "There's a freight elevator on the south side of the floor," she told them.

"Which way is south?" Boransky asked.

"Your left."

Sydney could see from the camera inside the elevator that it was an old model with slatted wooden doors. The team entered, aware that they would be exposed to each floor they passed.

"How slow is this thing?" Gudenov asked once the doors finally closed.

"Who cares?" Boransky snapped. "It beats the stairs."

"Petrova, lock out any externals," Anna ordered. "We don't want to have to stop for anyone."

"The elevator's too old," Sydney replied. "I don't have that kind of access." She dialed through the bank of cameras around the elevator on each floor. "There's a maid waiting on the seventh floor," she said, trying not to sound concerned.

"Let's take care of this," said Anna, and for one horrifying moment, Sydney thought they were going to kill the maid. Instead, she heard Velcro ripping and saw the team members peel off their coverall uniforms to reveal Kevlar vests emblazoned with MILITSIA, the Russian word for *POLICE*.

The elevator stopped. The doors opened. Five gun muzzles trained themselves on a confused sixty-year-old maid.

For a moment, the woman didn't seem to recognize what she was looking at. Sydney held her breath as Anna brought her finger to her lips. "Police business," Anna whispered. "For your protection, go to the nearest room and do not come out, do you understand?"

The terrified maid nodded and hurried down the hallway, leaving behind her rolling cart of toiler paper, towels, and soap. The doors closed and the team continued to the ninth floor. Sydney noticed something drip on her laptop.

It was a bead of sweat. She hadn't even realized she was perspiring.

Anna wedged the elevator door open with a wooden block and led the team to room 9071. She motioned to Sokolov, who placed two charges of putty at the points where the hinges would be on the other side. Then he ran wires connecting the globs of putty while Anna backed the rest of the team away.

Anna counted down with her fingers: three, two, one . . .

Sokolov blew the door. There was a huge flash but less of a bang than Sydney had been expecting.

Sokolov kicked the door down, letting Anna charge in. The feeds didn't extend into the rooms, so Sydney stared at an empty hallway, wondering what was going on.

She heard: "Freeze!"

She heard: "Drop it, drop it, drop it!"

She heard: "No biting. *Stop biting!*"

After ninety seconds, Anna and the rest of the team reappeared in the hallway. Sokolov and Boransky carried a body bag on their shoulders. And whatever was in the body bag was alive and *kicking*.

Sydney heard the sirens as Anna led her team back the way they had come. She checked the feed and saw armed guards approaching the elevator on the ground floor.

"We have a problem," Sydney called into her comm.

"Go ahead," Anna radioed back.

"Guards are waiting for you on the first floor."

"You said we had ten minutes," Sokolov protested.

"You *did*. It must have been the maid," Sydney said.

"Give us an alternate route, then," Anna barked. *"Quickly."*

"Go back to the other end of the hall," Sydney said. As they did, she focused the camera on the west side of the stairs. "There's a fire exit fifty feet ahead of you, do you see it?"

"We have to lug this thing down nine flights of stairs?" Boransky groaned. As if in reaction to this, the body started a fresh bout of kicking.

Sokolov leaned in to what Sydney could only

assume was the body's head. He hissed, "Comrade, don't make us drop you down these stairs. Because we will."

"Wait," Sydney said. "Back up." They stopped at a large trunk sitting beside a storage closet. "Open the trunk."

"We don't have time for this," Gudenov said.

"Just open it. Take everything out. You might be able to fit the body inside."

"What will that get us? More weight to carry around?" Anna found the camera Sydney was using and stared straight into it. Straight at Sydney.

Sydney forced herself to stay cool. "The police will be here in a minute, maybe less. You can't beat them. They'll be looking for four suspects in black tactical gear. They won't be looking for three men and a woman carrying a trunk. Dump your clothes and your weapons—"

"This is insane," Anna interrupted. "How are we going to be less of a target with this stupid trunk?"

But Sydney wouldn't let herself be stopped, her mind was racing too fast. "I'll stage a diversion. For the police and the guards. They won't even notice you. Just keep moving when you hear the fire alarms." She ripped off her comm headset and flew into the hotel. The delivery entrance was still unlocked from the team's initial break-in. So she quickly found the same stairwell Anna and her men had hit. But instead of going up, she went down.

She started in the basement, moving from the laundry room into the kitchen, pulling every fire alarm she saw. She followed a concrete corridor, where she passed two more fire alarms, until she wound up on the other side of the hotel. The waitstaff stared at her as she passed, not sure how to respond to the mechanical wailing that soon filled the basement.

"There's a fire on the seventh floor!" Sydney shouted at them. "Get out now!"

By the time she reached the ground level, the hotel lobby was flooded with people. The armed guards were joined by the arriving police in a vain attempt to stop the flow of people. Sydney couldn't go back through the delivery entrance. Instead, she joined the mass of humanity and walked out the front door. She was circling back to the delivery alley when the black van screeched up in front of her.

The door slid open and Sokolov leaned out, extending his hand. Sydney grabbed it and he yanked her inside, her knees skidding on the floor of the van. The door slid shut and the van pulled away. The team were out of their combat gear and had stripped down to nylon pants and gray T-shirts.

"Not bad, Petrova, not bad," Boransky said. "We may make an operative out of you yet." Sydney felt her heart pounding in her chest, the endorphin rush a primal release she'd almost forgotten she could have.

But when her eyes drifted down to the hostage, the rush turned to a wave of nausea. They'd left the trunk behind, naturally, and removed him from the body bag.

The subject was still bound and gagged, but there was a moment of recognition between them. Sydney suddenly realized she'd made a terrible, terrible mistake.

The man the team had kidnapped was Anatoly Gromnovich.

The light-headedness wouldn't go away. Sydney pitched forward, only to feel large hands grab her before she could hit the van floor. Sokolov's, she assumed before slipping into unconsciousness.

The last thing she heard was his guttural laugh. "I told you new bloods couldn't take it!"

9

IT WAS COMMON FOR agents, especially new agents, to suffer massive headaches. Graham had reassured Sydney, when she complained of migraines she thought were going to split her head open, that her brain was simply trying to absorb the stress she subjected it to when she went out on missions. "Some people throw up," he said. "A few suffer grand mal seizures. You get headaches. Once your body gets acclimated to the risks you take, your headaches will go away."

As Sydney slowly regained consciousness, her

senses had the usual cloudiness that resulted from passing out. But she didn't have a headache. Going over the events that had brought her here to begin with, she wondered if maybe Graham was right. Maybe she was getting used to this whole putting-your-life-in-peril thing.

When she opened her eyes, she wondered if she was dead.

She was suspended about three feet above the ground in a brilliant all-white environment. A part of her had always imagined heaven to be this white.

But the more she took in her surroundings, the more she doubted she was dead. Heaven probably didn't have a tile floor. Or fluorescent track lighting. And she definitely wouldn't be paralyzed in heaven.

She heard voices behind her. The first one she placed immediately: Gregoran.

"And that's all you know about her?" he asked.

"Everything else checks out." The second voice was impossibly low. The voices of Darth Vader, Barry White, and her father all rolled into one. "Her father is in the hospital, dying of cancer. Their records support her story."

"Check again."

"I've already run two checks. There's nothing unusual." The voices were getting closer. Sydney shut her eyes. She could feel the men approaching her. Then they were standing in front of her. She heard them breathing, smelled Gregoran's cologne.

"Is she awake?" Gregoran asked.

"She'll stay out for another two hours," the other man replied.

"No, she's awake."

Sydney heard a zipper open and suddenly she lost all sense of balance. The only thing she could be certain of was that she was falling. It was a short trip. She landed heavily on the floor.

"Welcome back to the land of the living, Sasha," Gregoran said above her. She squinted up into the brilliant lights to see the director of operations and the other man, who was, well . . .

He was a giant. There was no other way to explain it. At least seven feet tall, wearing a comically large lab coat that would swallow Sydney if she tried it on. He bent down, ignoring Gregoran's rudeness, and offered his hand. "Here," he said, "let me help you."

Sydney took it as she stood. Absently, she reached out for balance and grabbed the structure she'd been lying in, a hammock that had wrapped around her like a cocoon. As Sydney held on to it, she could feel her body heat dissipating from it.

"That's my living womb," the man said. "It holds

you in a slight fetal position, while supporting your head and neck. It guarantees you eight hours of the best sleep you've ever had." He gestured to the head support. "I had speakers installed at one point to play a heartbeat. But I took them out once test subjects started to cry when I woke them. And I don't mean just a few tears either. I'm talking *wailing*. Like they were being born all over again. Well, you get the idea."

The man put one enormous hand on Sydney's back to steady her. She appreciated it, since she still felt shaky. "Where are my manners?" he asked. "My name's Leo."

"S—" Sydney almost gave her own name. "Sasha," she said with a gulp. "Where am I?"

"My lab," Leo said, gesturing around them. "This is where I make things."

The first thing Sydney's eye was drawn to was an operating table. An animal she didn't recognize was splayed on it, its four—*five?*—paws pinned down and its torso cut open, the result of a crude autopsy. Beyond that were a series of mannequins, each of which had a different skin tone that appeared to be painted on. As Sydney's gaze focused, she saw a small bottle of dye next to each mannequin. *This guy is the K-Directorate equivalent of Graham,* she thought. *I'm not in psych op or in a holding cell. I'm in op-tech.*

"This is . . ." Sydney gasped. "This is amazing."

"Thanks." Leo smiled. "I like to think so."

"Yes," Gregoran harrumphed, "we're all very impressed." Turning to her, he said, "Sasha, you gave us quite a scare in the van. Is everything all right?"

Sydney tried to figure out how she'd ended up here instead of a holding cell. Maybe she'd miscalculated Gregoran's level of suspicion. Maybe he didn't want her dead after all.

"Was the mission a success?" she asked.

Gregoran sucked his teeth. "As a matter of fact, yes. The prisoner is being questioned as we speak."

"Turns out there was a breach in our network security," Leo said. "We have to upgrade the—"

"That's enough!" Gregoran snapped. Clearly Leo was about to explain something he wasn't supposed to. Even though he didn't get through it all, Sydney's heart hit the floor. She'd heard enough.

Gromnovich had broken.

He must have revealed the SD-9 plan for downloading the virus. *There we go, that's our mission. Abort, abort,* she thought. *He may not have revealed anything about Diana and me yet, but he will. They'll keep working on him.*

Gregoran kept his eyes on Sydney. "How much longer will you need to keep her here?" he asked Leo.

"Fifteen, twenty minutes," Leo replied. "Just

need to run some diagnostics." For Sydney's benefit, he added, "That's a computer joke."

Gregoran checked his watch. "It's five-thirty," he told her. "Your shift is over. Go home and get some rest so we can have you back bright and early tomorrow morning." His hand not so casually lingered on her back as he said this. Unlike Leo's, it wasn't to steady her. It was an attempt at an intimate gesture that succeeded only in repulsing Sydney.

Gregoran turned and walked out of Leo's lab. The doors hissed open and shut automatically for him. Leo rummaged around the lab. "You're in trouble," he said. "I think he likes you."

"Yes . . . lucky me."

"He sees many different women. But that's not entirely what I mean." Leo found what he was looking for. He pulled a remote control from one of the many drawers in his desk and pointed it at the camera in the corner of the room. The red Record light blinked off.

Sydney did a double take. "You . . . you turned the camera off."

"I did."

"That's against protocol! How did you do that?"

"One of the nice things about being a genius working for a company that wants to destroy democracy is that they allow me certain perks. Like my privacy."

Sydney stared at him, stunned. He wasn't content just to break protocol. He was breaking cover.

But why?

"Now listen very closely to me," Leo said. "Because there's only one way you're going to survive this, Sasha." He stopped and gave her a smile.

"Or should I call you Sydney?"

IT WAS RARE THAT Sydney's mind short-circuited, that she couldn't find a solution to a problem. But with Leo, she drew a blank.

"My—my name is Sasha," she said. But she couldn't sell her lie, not when he knew her real name.

"You talk in your sleep," Leo said. He pointed his remote at the ceiling. "Here, take a listen."

Over the speakers recessed in the ceiling, she heard her own voice. She sounded petulant, perhaps four years old. "But I don't *like* broccoli," she said.

The worst part was she'd said it in English.

"The living womb facilitates regression," Leo

said. "I've found out all kinds of things about people when they take a nap in it."

"But I don't *like* broccoli," the regressed Sydney said again over the speakers. Then she repeated it, as if she was having an argument with some unseen presence but had only one thing to say. "No," she whined. "I don't *like* broccoli."

"This goes on for a while," Leo told her. "In your case, it was easy to find out your name. I said, 'Who am I speaking to?' and you told me. After that, I ran a simple background check and found out about Credit Dauphine. Which is one of SD-6's suspected cover corporations.

"I'm guessing whatever you're planning involves our internal computer network," Leo continued. "What you should know is that I had to take the whole server offline because your man—what's his name? Gromnovich?"

"Leo, I really don't know what you're talking about."

Leo steamrolled over her. "Gromnovich told us about how you're going to bypass the biometric sensors. If you want to download something, you'll have to use my mainframe. It's the only one that's still online. The CCTV feeds are monitored from our security section," he explained. "But all the footage is digitized for review here. If you can knock out any of the cameras at this junction, it should set off a chain reaction that will knock out that second mainframe. Which means you'll take out the whole building."

* * *

Sydney made it back to her flat unscathed, though the walk from K-Directorate had made her feel like a fish in a barrel. She'd been convinced that at any moment a sniper would take her out from one of the Moscow skyscrapers, or that a car would slow down and the last thing she would see would be a gun muzzle. But nothing happened. Sydney forced herself not to freak out, not to grab her phone and immediately call Diana, not to go to the Screaming Boar and beg to be extracted.

She grabbed one of Francie's stars and rolled it between her fingers. It was an obsessive-compulsive trait, a desire to keep her hands busy while her mind worked through a problem. Francie had once watched, enthralled, as Sydney had dissected a piece of lettuce while studying for a test on *The Canterbury Tales*.

The bleating of her cell phone startled her in the silence of her apartment. She answered on the second ring.

"In two minutes a cab will pull up outside your

apartment." It was Diana. "Get in, and keep your head down." She hung up before Sydney could respond. They had to keep calls short so K-Directorate couldn't locate the cellular signal and listen in.

Ninety seconds later, Sydney waited on the curb outside her building. The sun had set, and night was descending on the city. She looked up and noticed that there were no stars in the sky, aside from the ones slowly moving across the horizon. Planes, she realized, taking off or landing at Moscow International Airport.

I travel halfway around the world and I get the same sky as Los Angeles, she thought. *I promised Francie I'd sleep under her stars. But all I see is darkness.*

Her heart sank as she thought of Francie back in the dorm. Sydney had never missed her friend as much as she did at that moment.

I'm sorry, her heart cried out. *I'm sorry for everything I did or didn't do. I'm sorry I couldn't be there for you when you needed me. I'm sorry I never got a chance to tell you how much I love you.*

I'm sorry, Francie! You don't have to forgive me, but you have to know I'm sorry!

The cab arrived, cutting off her thoughts. It didn't have a company name, just the basic yellow checkered design. She climbed in, and the cab screeched away as soon as she slammed the door. Sydney saw the faint glow of headlights following them. She turned around to catch a seventies-model Mercedes sedan keeping a safe distance but definitely on their tail.

"Can you lose these guys?" she asked the driver.

"I can," the driver responded. "But I won't."

She stared at him, perplexed. "Why not?'

"Because if I start driving like a bat out of hell," he said, "they'll have the evidence they need to prove you're a double agent. Now keep your head down. You're in SD-9's hands now."

They drove in silence for fifteen minutes. Sydney lost all her bearings. Finally she heard a whooshing noise get closer as the cab made a right turn and stopped.

Flap-flap . . . flap-flap . . . flap-flap . . . hssssss . . . whooooosh . . .

What was that?

The car started to inch forward. The streetlights gave way to total darkness.

Suddenly Sydney heard the driver's door open. "Good luck, Sasha" was all he said before he dashed away. Sydney sat up.

It was a car wash. The driver had pulled into a car wash.

The flapping noise came from the large black

plastic flaps that the car swept under before getting doused with jets of water and soap. Sydney noticed streaks of yellow paint pouring down the windows.

When the taxi emerged from the other end of the car wash, she caught a glimpse of what happened in the reflection of a window. The yellow paint job was gone, as were any markings that designated the car as a taxi. If the car passed you on the street, you would hardly notice it. It was just another basic white vehicle in busy Moscow traffic.

A new driver climbed into the front seat and Sydney ducked back down. She sat there in silence for two minutes as she felt the car pull back into traffic.

Finally, she heard a deep sigh from the front seat and the new driver called out, "All right, you can sit up."

She did, and she was not entirely surprised to see that the new driver was Diana.

* * *

Twenty minutes later, they were walking toward the satellite dishes. "Am I clean?" Diana asked. Sydney thought the question was directed toward her, but Diana had turned away, seemingly getting an answer from somewhere else.

She turned back to Sydney, nodded that it was okay to talk, and led her to the radio-silent area. "Okay," she asked, "what did Leo tell you?"

Sydney took a deep breath. And then she told Diana everything that had happened in the lab.

"Oh God." Diana exhaled loudly. "This is a disaster."

"There was no way for me to maintain my alias," Sydney said. "I didn't have a choice. But I think Leo might want to help us."

"How can you be sure?" Diana snapped. "Did Arvin Sloane not explain who you were dealing with? This isn't some two-bit terrorist outfit, this is *K-Directorate*!" Sydney had never seen this side of Diana. She hadn't even thought that it existed in a woman as cool and collected as her handler had been up to this point.

"I asked them to send me the best!" Diana yelled—she was yelling now. "And who do they send me? Some nineteen-year-old who, at the beginning of the day, helps capture my handler, and at the end of the day, *blows her cover by talking in her sleep*!"

Sydney closed her eyes and counted to three. It was all she could do to keep from crying. But the tears came anyway, brimming in her eyes, refusing to fall.

"I'll give you two ways I can be sure Leo wants to

help us," Sydney answered, her voice uneven. "First, he let me go. If Leo were loyal to K-Directorate, neither of us would be standing here."

Diana glared at her but said nothing. "What's the second reason?" she asked after a few seconds.

"He told me details," Sydney said. "Details that could help us see this mission through."

"Like what?" Diana demanded.

"Well, if, um, if we want to download something, we have to use his mainframe. It's the only one that's still online." She gulped some air. "And the CCTV feeds are monitored from his security section."

"That makes sense," Diana said, still fuming. "We were told today that the network was being beefed up and nobody would be able to do anything until the end of the day tomorrow."

She wasn't exactly warming up to the idea of trusting Leo, but she was listening. "What else?"

"The CCTV feeds run through a junction in his wing. Knock one out and we blind the whole system," Sydney finished, with a small shrug.

Diana studied her. "I'll run that by SD-9 op-tech," Diana said. "But it might be true. I'm not familiar enough with the security systems to know for sure."

Then Diana took hold of her arm. "Why did he tell you all this?"

Sydney had wondered the same thing. In fact, she had come right out and asked him.

"Do you know what I do for K-Directorate?" he had asked in return. "I follow orders and give them things like this." He had pulled out a metal sphere the size of a baseball. He'd depressed a button, set it on the autopsy table. "Duck."

"What?"

"Duck!" Leo had insisted, pulling her down. Sydney had felt a rush of air above her head. When Leo had helped her back to her feet, she'd noticed little pins sticking in the walls in a circle around the room.

"All they want from me are new and efficient ways of killing people," he had said. "And I'm tired of it."

He'd plucked one of the needles from the wall and pressed it into Sydney's hand until it pricked her skin, leaving a small trickle of blood in her palm. "If you're sabotaging K-Directorate, I want to be a part of it. And when you leave, I want you to take me with you."

"He wants to defect?" Diana asked, breathless, after Sydney explained it to her.

"Yes."

Diana weighed this. "SD-9 could use somebody like him."

"I know," Sydney smiled. "He'd finally be working for the good guys."

"Did he tell you anything else?"

Sydney nodded. "That Gromnovich was in a room and was being torn down. They—" she took a deep breath. "They were climbing the Ladder."

Diana absorbed this. They stood in silence and Sydney's handler rubbed her eyes. She was crying.

Diana knew about the Ladder. And so did Sydney.

Part of training as a spy was learning counter-intelligence resistance—how to survive torture. The most widely used technique taught agents how to steel their minds against questioners. It organized into levels the intelligence they would allow themselves to reveal, depending on the duress they were subjected to.

This technique was called the Ladder.

The first rung involved mentally compiling the list of false information you had memorized before you left for the mission. The second rung was giving the lowest level of harmful secrets. If your torturers threaten to cut off a finger, you give them dummy codes to nuclear weapons. If they shoot you in the foot, you give them names of spies who exist only on paper. The philosophy, Sydney remembered, was based on a weird fusion of Zen Buddhism and Lamaze. You trick your brain into disassociating from the pain by revealing intel you know won't lead anywhere.

And if they continued to try to break you, you continued up the Ladder until you started giving them *real* intelligence. The higher rungs involved revealing the locations of weapons stashes or future missions. The former usually didn't cause much collateral damage, and the latter could always be aborted. The top rung of the Ladder was giving your enemy the names of other agents.

When one organization questioned a member of another, they assumed that the first few hours' worth of intelligence the enemy gave them was rubbish. Their goal was always to reach the top of the Ladder. And in this case, sitting at the top of the Ladder were Sydney and Diana. Sydney couldn't help wondering, if it had taken K-Directorate six hours to get as far as they did on the grizzled spy, how long would it take before they made it the rest of the way?

But Diana wasn't crying because of the risks she and Sydney faced. She was crying because her handler was nothing if not tough. For K-Directorate to have made such progress, Gromnovich must have been in unimaginable pain.

"We can't do it," Diana announced. She hadn't simply been weeping for her friend. She'd been processing their options. Diana was nothing if not efficient.

"Why not?"

"I don't have the op-tech," Diana said. "It'll take weeks for SD-9 to figure out how to disrupt the CCTV units. Unless you can somehow deliver a miracle."

Sydney hesitated, feeling like a fifth grader who was afraid to raise her hand even though she knew the answer. "What if I told you I could?"

* * *

Sydney and Diana had been under the satellite dishes for hours, poring over every detail of the mission.

"Okay, so if you are able to knock the cameras out and download HYDRA," Diana said, repeating the last pieces of their newly hatched plan, "that will give me the cover I need to rescue Gromnovich." She paused. "All of security has to be distracted or I won't be able to get into the cell block."

"What if I make them come to Leo's lab?" Sydney asked.

"What do you mean?"

"Stage a diversion that they have to respond to."

Diana mulled this over. "The only variable is Leo."

"We paint the crime scene to exonerate him. Make sure K-Directorate knows he's innocent. Then we extract him tomorrow night."

"Assuming we get out alive."

"Yes."

Diana nodded. It *could* work. "Okay. How do you propose whitewashing our good friend Leo?"

Sydney handed Diana the hypodermic pen Graham had given her back in L.A. "Get ready for miracle number two."

* * *

Forty-five minutes later, Diana parked the car five blocks from Sydney's apartment building. "This is as close as I can get you without K-Directorate picking us up," Diana said.

"That's okay," Sydney said. "I need to clear my head anyway, to get all the details straight for tomorrow."

Diana drummed her fingers on the steering wheel. "You know, this isn't the mission you signed up for. If you want to be extracted now, tonight, no one would blame you."

Sydney thought about Sloane and the look of confidence on his face when he briefed her for the mission. She thought of Noah, who had risked his life to ensure she got her shot here.

And she thought of Francie, sitting all alone in the

dorm, unless the Parkers had whisked her off to New Mexico again.

You do this job, she told herself, *so people like Francie can sleep at night. So they don't have to worry about, or even know about, places like K-Directorate.*

"I came this far," Sydney answered. "I want to see it through."

Diana nodded. "I guess there's only one question left." And, surprising Sydney, Diana burst into laughter before asking, "What is *that*?"

Sydney looked down. She had started rolling one of Francie's glow-in-the-dark stars in her fingers again. She'd been doing it since the satellite dishes.

"It's nothing," she said. "Something a friend gave me before the mission. A good luck charm." She paused, inspecting it, then repeated, "It's nothing, it's stupid."

Diana took it from her and held it up. "Well, if it's stupid, can I have it?"

Sydney almost laughed herself. "Why?"

"Because right now we could use all the luck we can get."

Sydney thought about it. "It's yours."

Diana slipped it into her pocket.

"I guess if this mission goes as planned," Sydney ventured, "we won't see each other again."

"That's sort of how it works," Diana said. "You do your half, I'll do mine. And we get out of there."

Sydney extended her hand to shake Diana's. "Good luck, I guess."

Diana looked at Sydney's hand, but didn't take it. After an uncomfortable silence, Sydney got out of the car, suddenly feeling childish.

"My name . . ." Diana called out, halting Sydney before the door could slam. Then, after another awkward moment, Diana tried again.

"My name is Demetria."

Sydney smiled, trying not to cry. "Nice to meet you."

Diana nodded. Sydney shut the door and watched the car disappear into the night.

I've been deep cover for forty-eight hours and I think I'm going to go crazy, she thought. *No Francie. No Noah. No Sloane. But how long has Diana been here? How long has it been since she talked to somebody who could ground her?*

She couldn't answer those questions.

But the more she tried to push them out of her head, the darker the questions became. In ten years, Diana had gone from an untrained revolutionary to the perfect spy, who afforded herself no personal connections, not even her own name. In another ten years, who would Diana be? Would she turn into one of Them, as Gromnovich had?

For that matter, would Sydney?

She stared up at the starless night again. "Sydney," she whispered, before heading toward her apartment building.

11

SYDNEY SAT AT HER desk, staring at random video images from around the city as they streamed by on her computer screen. A stack of surveillance reports lay in her in-box, but it was useless to think about work. With her right hand, she traced a pattern on the numeric pad of her keyboard.

137.60.4529 . . . 137.60.4529 . . . 137.60.4529 . . .

It was the IP server address to Graham's HYDRA virus. She'd spent half an hour the night before training the pattern of the numbers into her fingers, getting the muscle memory down so that she wouldn't hesitate when she had to enter the real thing.

She looked up at the clock on her computer: 10:27.

Ten twenty-eight was the agreed-upon time when she and Diana would begin their mission. She could either wait forty-five seconds or she could get a head start. She opted to get the head start.

She pushed back from her desk and walked down the corridor to Leo's office. The women's bathroom was also this way. Nobody's eyebrows would rise if they saw her leave—at least, that's what she told herself. She pulled out her Taser-phone and palmed it. She was twenty yards away from the camera that swerved back and forth at a forty-five degree angle.

Don't look at the camera, Don't look at the camera, Don't look at the camera, she chanted to herself. But her gait picked up slightly as she positioned herself directly under the camera before it could capture her onscreen.

Once she was in position, she stretched out the hand holding the Taser, reached toward the camera, and entered the firing code. The two needles shot from the phone and stuck hard to the camera, penetrating its metal housing. Thirty thousand volts shot into it. Sydney smelled ozone as the camera's circuitry overloaded and melted. She pressed the pound button again and the Taser wires popped from the phone to hang lifelessly against the wall.

Sydney glanced around the corner. Another camera at the end of the hall was dead, its red light off. The whole wing was down. And if what Leo had told her was correct, so was the rest of the building.

The door to Leo's lab hissed open and she entered. Leo's back was to her. He sat on a stool, his giant frame hunched over a microscope.

"Somebody's disturbing my no visitors policy," he growled without looking up. "Unless you're my mother or a beautiful girl, leave me alone."

"Leo—"

He stood, turned, saw who it was, and grinned. "Wow. You don't have a million rubles, do you? I meant, a beautiful girl with a million rubles . . ."

"Leo, it's happening."

His grin faded. "What—"

"You want to get out of here, don't you?"

"Now?"

"Tonight. But first, you have to help me."

Leo ran to a bank of monitors embedded in the wall. He flipped through several channels. "What about the cameras?"

"They're out." Sure enough, the monitors displayed only static.

He glared at her, annoyed. "Would it have killed you to give me a little advance notice?"

"There wasn't any time. I need your help to

download a virus. Once we do that, we'll be able to extract you."

He moved over to his mainframe. On the floor in front of the machine was a vipers' nest of wires. He plunged his hand into the overlapping coil and pulled out a keyboard. "This is wrong," he muttered. "There are a hundred better ways to do this."

She would have looked over his shoulder as he plugged the keyboard into a port on the computer, but she wasn't tall enough. Instead, she peered around his elbow. "Can you get me to a UNIX prompt?"

His hands flew over the keys. She watched closely as he entered a series of commands and a UNIX Internet window popped up.

"What's the address?"

She reached around him and typed it in herself. It was faster than telling him. The monitor read:

HYDRA.EXE

DOWNLOADING . . . 3% COMPLETE

APPROXIMATE TIME REMAINING: 4:56

Brrring! It was the phone in his lab. "That," Leo said, "would be security, wondering why the CCTV feeds are down."

"You can't answer it," Sydney said.

Brrring!

"I have to. If I don't, they'll send someone down to investigate."

Brrring!

Sydney felt her pulse begin to quicken. "And if you do, you'll have to find an excuse that we can back up."

Brrring!

"So?"

"So unless our story is completely convincing, they'll be watching you like a hawk. We won't be able to extract you."

Brrring!

"I'm answering the phone."

"Leo, no—" But with three giant strides, he was already halfway to it. She couldn't stop him. Instead, she began rummaging through the drawers and cabinets in his lab.

"This is Leo," he said, feigning casualness.

She found what she needed in a small closet next to the mainframe. A crowbar. That would work.

"What?" Leo shouted into the phone. "What are you talking about?"

It was about this time that he noticed Sydney approaching—stalking him, really. He began to look scared—at least, as legitimately scared as a seven-foot-giant could be of a five-foot-nine-inch nineteen-year-old wielding a crowbar.

"What are you doing?" he demanded. "Put down

that crowbar." Whoever he'd been talking to on the phone must have been very confused. But that was okay. It would work to Sydney's advantage.

Sydney raised the crowbar and brought it smashing down.

Leo flinched, but the crowbar didn't even come close to hitting him.

No, she was aiming for the phone. The cradle exploded into a hundred pieces, scattering plastic all over the tile floor.

"Now K-Directorate will think somebody came into your office, smashed your phone, and downloaded the virus," Sydney said.

"They'll give me a lie detector test," he said softly. "Don't you get it? When they find me here, they'll know I saw something. And the test? I designed it myself. It reads brain activity, Sydney. *There's no way to outsmart it!*"

"That's not true," Sydney said quietly. "There is one way."

She reached into her pocket and pulled out the hypodermic pen. She pressed the button so that the needle stuck out. "This contains a cocktail that knocks you out and wipes your short-term memory clean."

He stared at the pen, the cold logic clicking into

place. "The only way I can avoid K-Directorate's scrutiny," he whispered, "is if I really don't know what happened."

"That's right," Sydney replied.

"Will I remember meeting you?"

"I don't know," she said. But she had trouble lying to him. "I don't think so." She read the doubt in his face and did her best to reassure him. "My handler and I went over every facet of this mission. This is the only way we can help you escape. I promise we won't leave you behind."

"But if you break that promise," Leo said, "I'll never remember it."

"Leo, please," she begged. "We don't have much time."

He stood up and handed her the pen. "There's something I have to do first." He walked over to his automatic door, found a small lever on the side, and pulled it down. Sydney watched, surprised, as a reinforcing barrier descended into the crack where the doors came together. "There," he said. "That will keep the guards out and buy you some time."

Three seconds later, pounding came on the door. "Leo, are you in there?" muffled voices called out. "What's going on?"

He took a deep breath and nodded. "Do it."

Sydney swung the pen in a sideways arc. A pen

tip appeared, then was replaced with the hypodermic needle. She swung the pen in a sideways arc, purposely aiming for a fleshy part of the body. On a woman, she would have aimed for the hips. But on Leo, the point of entry was his stomach.

The needle entered smoothly, injecting the drug into his system as soon as it was depressed into the skin. Leo staggered, his body already betraying him. He stumbled into his own CCTV mainframe, holding on to it for support. It didn't help him. He slid down against it, somehow turning his massive bulk over to stare at Sydney. She was frozen. *Don't forget me,* his gaze said.

And then the memory-erasing drugs were already taking effect. A slow bewilderment spread over him. He looked down at the needle/pen sticking out of his gut, then back up at Sydney, as if to say, *Isn't that weird?*

And then he passed out.

Sydney ran to the network mainframe to check her progress.

She nearly screamed.

HYDRA.EXE

DOWNLOADING . . . 2% COMPLETE

APPROXIMATE TIME REMAINING: 4:58

It was *slowing down.* The next time she looked, the screen read:

28% COMPLETE

APPROXIMATE TIME REMAINING: 3:48

Then:

15% COMPLETE

APPROXIMATE TIME REMAINING: 4:00

and:

42% COMPLETE

APPROXIMATE TIME REMAINING: 2:40

The estimated time jumped wildly, like a broken speedometer. There was no way to tell how long she had.

"Leo, we're coming through!" the voices yelled. "Back away from the door!"

Sydney vaulted on top of the mainframe. She removed a ceiling panel and grabbed the pipes above her head. She tested them for a brief instant, making sure they could hold her weight. Then she wrapped herself around the pipes. Hanging by her knees, she replaced the panel she'd dislodged just as she heard a crash below her. It wasn't explosives; it sounded as if the guards were trying to break through the doors.

She crawled along the pipes for two hundred feet until she reached what had to be the women's bathroom. Along the way, she glanced down at the pinpoint holes in the paneling to see people in a slight daze walking through the halls, in and out of offices.

Everybody knew something was wrong; a few

even pointed to cameras, noticing that the ever-blinking lights were off. But for the most part, there was an eerie calm over the place. It wasn't the like the response to a fire alarm, when shock was followed by a frantic rush. This was the whisper of a coworker's suicide or a boss's meltdown, the unease that everybody felt but no one could put their finger on.

Sydney made it back to the bathroom, which, she could see from her vantage point, was empty. She removed a ceiling panel and dropped onto the room-length marble sink. After carefully replacing the panel, she jumped to the floor and walked out of the bathroom. With a little luck, she might be able to exit the building without being noticed.

Blink.

The cameras' red lights blinked back on.

"All employees, report to the central auditorium," boomed the PA. *"Repeat, all employees, report to the central auditorium."*

Sydney held her breath as K-Directorate employees began pouring through doors from other wings. She was swimming against the tide to reach the exit, but she was so close. If she could just get to the stair-well . . .

A guard cut her off. He held his M-16 across his chest and stepped in front of her. "The central auditorium is the other way," he said.

Sydney looked beyond him. The exit was yards away. "I forgot my purse," she bluffed.

"Get it later."

She sized him up like a piece of meat. He was chubby, slow. Without the gun, there wouldn't have been a question.

Except he wasn't alone. Other guards began to dot the hallway. They kept their eyes on the crowd, looking for an excuse to break some heads. Sydney's would do just fine.

"Right." Sydney exhaled. "Who needs lip gloss anyway?"

12

SYDNEY LOOKED AROUND, agog. Could this many people really be working for K-Directorate?

The auditorium was a gigantic oval, with a speaking pit in the center. She slipped in quietly next to Mina and the rest of her coworkers from her wing. Guards directed the rest of the employees to their pre-assigned standing positions. Above them all, in a balcony that circled the room, were black-suited men, none younger than fifty, all frowning down at the proceedings.

"What's going on?" Sydney whispered to Mina.

"Somebody got caught," Mina whispered back.

"Who?"

"Who knows?"

"What were they caught doing?"

"Does it matter?" Mina asked. "I hear the reason we're in assigned positions is so they can just press a button."

"Press a button?"

The lights dimmed.

"You know. They press a button, the floor opens up, and *whoosh*. One of us goes straight down into the crocodile pit."

Sydney took the low lighting as an opportunity to scope out an emergency exit. But two guards were posted at each door. And there was no way to move in the stillness without distracting everybody. She began to see the cold logic of the circle. With all those eyes peering down from above, no one could escape.

A spotlight illuminated the speaking pit in the center. Gregoran entered and cleared his throat.

"Rumor control," he announced in his striking tenor. "We have summoned you here to conduct *rumor control*."

The crowd of employees, who had been slumped in their standing position, suddenly stood at attention.

"You all promised loyalty to K-Directorate," he proclaimed. "And you've all been informed of the penalty of certain offenses. The only way . . ." He paused, taking in the crowd. With one sweeping glare, he seemed to make contact with everyone in the room. "The *only* way we can be effective as an intelligence organization is if we embrace the truth. This is why, when an incident occurs—when people start whispering in the hallways—we must join together here. And we must conduct *rumor control*."

He's preaching, Sydney realized. If she had any doubt that this man was Josef, that he could hold an audience in his hands, it disappeared in that instant.

"But, friends, not all of you have been honest with us. Someone among you, someone in *this very room,* has infiltrated our workplace. Has *corrupted* this family." Gregoran moved out from the speaking pit and began drifting into the crowd. The spotlight followed him. "Ladies and gentlemen, when a cancer invades your body, what do the doctors tell you? They say . . ."

He faced one of the workers. He seemed to know her. "They say, 'Ilya, the first thing we must do is *identify* the cancer.' "

He moved on to the next woman. "They say, 'Mildred, we have to isolate the cancer.' "

He stood before an overweight video tech who worked three cubicles down from Sydney. "They say, 'Boris, we must *cut out* the cancer. Cut it out in order to *kill it*.' "

Sydney felt panic surging inside her. *They're*

going to kill somebody right here. Just like Anna was going to kill Aleksander. Only this time, they're going to go through with it.

Gregoran's voice rooted her to her spot. "The person who committed this crime against us is a recent hire who used charm as a *smokescreen*. To do what?" When the audience didn't reply, he raised his voice to a minister's scream. "I ask you, *to do what?*"

The words reverberated throughout the space. If the arena had been a church, people might have shouted a reply, catching his spirit. But no one dared to say anything in this hallowed circle. "To assault our security systems," he said, answering his own question in a stage whisper. "To compromise us from the inside."

Gregoran began to wade down Sydney's aisle. *This is it,* Sydney thought. *Diana performed her half of the mission, and she got luckier than I did. She and Gromnovich got out. I'm the one they have trapped.*

"It began with an attack on our camera systems." Gregoran walked toward the cluster of video techs and strolled menacingly from worker to worker. "That was followed by an attempt to infect our computer network." He spun, raising a finger in the air. "But thanks to the quick wits of our IS department, that attempt failed! We will not let those enemies of our state corrupt us! You heard the rumors—now hear the truth!"

He turned his attention back to the video tech employees, probing each one for some sort of weakness.

"The attacker was *young*," he shouted. Karl, the pale, frightened man who stood before Gregoran, was in his forties. Gregoran moved on.

"The attacker was *female*." Gregoran now stood in front of Mina. He took a long, hard look at her. Mina couldn't help it. She began to tremble.

It was Sydney's worst nightmare come horribly to life.

She had downloaded HYDRA. She was guilty. Gregoran knew it just by looking at her. She was convinced that everyone else did as well.

"The attacker was beautiful," he finished. "And she fooled us all."

Sydney opened her mouth to speak.

"Surely, Pietr, you didn't bring us all here without firm evidence to back up your claims."

The words didn't come from her. They came from Diana. Sydney recognized the voice before she found the person, who was somewhere in the dark auditorium. Another spotlight blazed to life, searching the circle crazily, trying to find the source of this insulting interruption.

It found her. Diana leaned against the wall of the auditorium, arms folded, perpetual smirk on her face.

Everything about her body language said, *I'm not impressed with you, Pietr. I never was.*

"I mean"—Diana chuckled—"isn't this rumor control?"

"Indeed it is," Gregoran replied. The preacher's tone was gone. He gave an imperceptible nod to somebody off to his left.

A tiny red light cut through the darkness. For a discombobulated moment, Sydney thought somebody had brought one of those annoying laser pointers fourteen-year-olds invariably found amusing to point at a movie screen.

But it was a laser *sighting*. The kind special operatives used on night missions to ensure they didn't miss their targets when they pulled the trigger.

The rifle report was sharp and quick. Sydney caught the muzzle flash, which briefly lit up the dark curly hair and lush mocha skin of the shooter.

Sydney's head whirled. *Who was it?* she asked herself. *Who took the hit?* But a part of her already knew.

"We encourage all nonrated agents to take the day off and reflect on this error in judgment. Tomorrow, we'll hold interviews to ensure that the cancer hasn't spread past this unfortunate incident. Thank you." Gregoran made a wrap-up motion with his hand.

The lights came up. A random scream rose above

the mumbling crowd, followed by a second, oddly, from the opposite side of the room. A few more short yelps erupted like popcorn. Then they began in earnest: a tag team of screams. One person would stop and another would start.

That's when Sydney saw her.

Diana was slumped against the wall, her eyes still open, a neat bullet hole in the center of her forehead.

Gregoran stood in front of Sydney. "She was young," he said quietly. "She was female And she was a recent hire. We had our suspicions from the beginning."

Sydney wheeled away from him. "She . . . she . . ."

"I know she was your handler and I'm sorry." Gregoran was actually trying to seem sincere. "Sasha, you're not under suspicion. Do you understand? I know you're loyal."

He's lying to you. He suspects you. This is all a test. You're still being judged. They want to see how quickly you fall apart after they kill your handler.

"I—I have to go," Sydney babbled. "I have to . . . I have to go home." At that moment, she meant home to Los Angeles. She wanted to go back to her room at UCLA, crawl under the covers, and not get up again until she turned, oh, thirty.

People flew past them. Some were actually running. All averted their eyes from the corpse on the floor. Everyone had had the same visceral reaction: to leave before K-Directorate shot them, too.

But Gregoran wouldn't let Sydney go. He held her arm in an *I'm there for you* gesture. "If you need to talk . . . ," he said meaningfully, letting the rest hang there.

Sydney fought to keep from slapping him.

When she pulled away a second time, he let her go. Tears blurred her vision as she staggered toward what she hoped was the exit.

But a strange sight, even through the tears, stopped her.

It was Anna.

She had moved across the auditorium to crouch over Diana's body. She was inspecting her kill. Sydney wanted to scream, *Get away from her! Don't touch her!* But she didn't. Instead, she watched as Anna reached down and plucked something from Diana's hand.

It was Sydney's glow star. The one she'd given Diana the night before.

Anna inspected it, confused as to what it was. Then, figuring it out, Anna smiled.

Anna smiled.

Sydney headed for the door and didn't look back.

13

SYDNEY STUMBLED THROUGH THE hallway, tears falling down her cheeks. *Diana is dead,* she thought dully, the vision of her friend slumped on the floor burning through her brain. *It could have been me. It should have been me!*

Somehow Mina found her, and together they joined the somber procession of employees walking up several flights of stairs.

"Are you going to be okay?" Mina asked when they got outside the building.

Sydney nodded. She needed to get to the Screaming Boar. She needed to get extracted.

Except that she'd be leaving Leo.

She rationalized it a hundred ways, but there was no getting around that fact. Yes, her smartest move would be to ensure her own safety, tell SD-9 that Leo wanted to defect, and have faith that they would get him out. But she couldn't depend on faith anymore. She couldn't depend on anything.

She had no idea how much later it was before she stared up at the familiar wooden sign of the spear-pierced boar—an hour? Maybe two? She walked in, the calm and darkness a welcome relief from the clamor and blinding sun of the Moscow day.

"Scotch," she said. Her tongue felt leaden in her mouth. "The twelve-year-old."

The bartender poured it without comment while a question pounded Sydney's brain. *Why did Diana come back?*

The plan had been simple: each was to perform her half of the mission. Each was to assume the other could take care of herself and escape safely. So what did Diana do?

They'd suspected her for a while, Gregoran had said. Diana herself must have been aware of that. But the assembly in the auditorium had been a public witch hunt. Gregoran had made a summary judgment and proceeded with a spot execution, courtesy of Anna. It hadn't been an issue of fairness or evidence.

It had been a snap decision meant to strike fear in the hearts of everyone in the office. Until Diana had reappeared, Sydney must have been the one they had picked out. She had seen it in Gregoran's eyes.

So why had she been lucky? And why had Diana come back?

With a shaking hand, Sydney put her coaster over her drink and retreated to the bathroom. *Some spy you turned out to be,* she thought as she pushed open the door.

* * *

Thirty minutes later, Sydney was still sitting in the bathroom stall.

Where *were* they?

Her mind played a loop of worst-case scenarios. SD-9 agents in a car, unsuspecting, as Anna's van pulled up behind them. The Spetsnaz team loading their automatic weapons, prepping for the hit. Anna's instructions: "After this, we go after Petrova."

Sydney couldn't stay in here any longer. With every second she remained in the bathroom stall, she only made herself an easier target. But never in her life had the world outside seemed so threatening.

What was it Sloane had said? That she excelled on missions where she could come up with her own solutions in a high-pressure scenario? Sydney gave the toilet paper a spin. She wasn't excelling now, that was for sure. She took a deep breath, opened the stall door, and walked out of the bathroom. *Pay for your drink,* she told herself, *and get out.*

But the first sign that something was wrong was that her glass was empty. And the second was the drunk who intercepted her as she dropped a bill on the bar.

"I'm . . . I'm sssorry," he slurred, holding on to both her and the bar for balance. "That drink was . . . sssitting there for so long . . . I thought you'd given up."

Sydney took a few defensive steps backward. "No, that's all right, I—"

He fell into her, pressing something small and circular into her stomach. *It's a bomb!* her mind screamed. *It's a bio-weapon!*

But it wasn't a bomb. It was a CD. Sydney palmed it and slid it under her shirt as the grizzled man apologized profusely, making a show of dusting her off.

"How many times do I have to tell you to stop harassing my customers!" the bartender shouted at him.

The drunk turned back to Sydney, shrugged, and smiled. "There's no room for gentlemen left in the world," he said. And suddenly Sydney placed him—he was the cabdriver from the night before.

He took a few steps back to let her pass. With a hint of what sounded like true concern, he said, "You take care of yourself."

Sydney nodded. She left without looking back.

* * *

It was a beautiful afternoon in Gorky Park. A family laughed as they struggled to get a kite in the air. A young couple snuggled on a picnic blanket. Joggers and rollerbladers gave each other plenty of space. Nobody noticed the distraught young woman sitting on a bench, slipping a CD into the player she'd bought from a leering pawn shop owner moments before.

"Sydney, this is Arvin Sloane." The voice was so reassuring she almost burst into tears. "We've been made aware of your situation. We're pursuing every avenue possible to ensure a safe extraction."

Sydney squeezed her eyes shut. Things were going to be all right. Sloane would be able to help. People were working to get her out of the country. They'd just gotten delayed, that's all.

"However . . ." Sloane paused. The hope that had been surging inside her took a nosedive. "We've been informed that SD-9 will not cooperate with us."

She heard the words, but they didn't compute.

SD-9 will not cooperate.

What did that mean?

Had she been sold out? Was she being punished?

"There was another component to your mission that we didn't detail in your briefing," Sloane said. "At the time, it was need-to-know-only information. The HYDRA virus that you were to download onto K-Directorate's network was actually a clone."

A clone of what?

"K-Directorate had infected SD-9 with a similar virus first. And because our computer systems are linked, they may have found a back door into the entire SD network." Sydney leaned forward slowly, letting her head rest in her hands. "We were hoping that by infecting K-Directorate with a version of their virus, we might obtain the necessary time to repair the damage. The other offices feel this is a top priority since the impact on our collective systems could be catastrophic."

Sloane paused. Sydney could hear the emotion in his voice. "Sydney, somehow we will get you out of there. But for now, you must maintain your alias. You must return to K-Directorate."

How could he say that? He didn't have to watch her handler get killed. He didn't have to face the judging eyes of the director of operations. *I can't do this!* she wanted to scream at him. *The mission is a failure. I can't maintain it. I can't go back!*

"Compounding the problem is that K-Directorate surveillance is unlike anything we've ever studied. Checkpoints throughout the city have you on a watch list. Biometric readings have scanned your facial dimensions into every camera in the area. Which means breaking your cover is a practical impossibility."

I know the systems, I trained on them. And right now, some tech geek has trained a low-Earth orbit satellite or traffic camera on me. Watching me try not to cry on a park bench while I listen to a CD.

"We understand that you'll be under even more intense scrutiny since your handler sacrificed herself. But your safest option is to weather the suspicion. . . ."

Sydney tuned Sloane out, a question burning in her mind. How had Sloane come by all this information so quickly? The answer, once she thought about it, was obvious.

There were other people involved in this plan. One had had his memory erased. One was dead. The third was Sydney. The process of elimination left one suspect: Gromnovich.

Diana must have released him and told him their plan before doubling back to hear Gregoran's speech, already in progress.

Distracted, Sydney pressed the Reverse button on the CD player and listened to Sloane's words again.

". . . since your handler sacrificed herself . . ."

Sacrificed. Sloane was always precise in his words. *Sacrificed.*

Diana came back for me. She knew I'd be killed, so she gave Gregoran a bigger target instead.

Sydney caught the tail end of Sloane's instructions. ". . . your own protection, you have to destroy any traces of evidence that might prove you are not who you say you are. Get rid of all SD-6 op-tech. Do it now, Sydney, before K-Directorate can find it."

She felt all the blood drain from her face. She had forgotten all about it. The SD-6 op-tech. She had the cell phone with her, but she had hidden the fingerprint inside a box of tea bags that Mrs. Andropov had pressed into her hands after dinner. There was no way the apartment could withstand a full-blown search by K-Directorate. She could imagine them now, tearing her flat apart while she wasted time listening to Sloane.

"Good luck, Sydney," Sloane's voice concluded.

She flew off the park bench, dodged around the family flying the kite, and jumped over the lovers on the grass. She slipped the CD from its player and snapped it in half. She threw one half in a garbage can and the other half in a Dumpster eight blocks away.

It was a mile and a half back to her apartment. She ran past the broken security doors, bolted up the four flights of stairs, and came to a screeching halt when she arrived at her landing.

Sokolov stood at her door. Sokolov from Anna's Spetsnaz team. Sokolov, who'd spun the knife on his palm. He was hunched over her lock, electric lock pick in hand, trying to break into her apartment. She stood there for a few seconds, panting.

"That's my apartment" was all she could finally manage to say.

Sokolov bolted upright. For some reason, he was standing at attention. But not because of her.

There were footsteps approaching from behind. And a quiet cough. Sydney turned to meet the hypnotic eyes of Pietr Gregoran.

"I was hoping," he said, "to have a chat with you."

* * *

Gregoran stopped Sokolov at the door after Sydney unlocked it. "Leave us."

Sokolov shifted uncertainly. "That's against protocol."

Gregoran glanced at him, annoyed. "If she turns out to be dangerous, I think I can handle her." He closed the door in his agent's face, then took in Sydney's apartment. "What's that smell?"

She opened the window. "The previous occupant let something die in here."

"Two or three somethings, it seems." He sat down in Sydney's sole chair.

"Tea?" she offered.

"Please." She crossed into the kitchen and grabbed the fingerprint when she took a tea bag out of the box. She slipped it into her pocket as she filled a pot with water.

"Diana's death was a shock to us all," Gregoran commented casually, as if he hadn't played a role in it. "Her rise within K-Directorate happened too quickly. It was too easy. Her missions were so successful, it was like somebody had handed her the answers. We like to see our agents struggle a little more to reach the top. Struggling keeps us honest."

Whatever, pal. Just keep talking. And don't get up. But she nodded as if she believed every word.

Gregoran added. "And it reinforces the message that in the spy game, as in life, there are no easy answers. But there was something that made Diana's rise to the top unique."

"What's that?"

"We don't believe she was acting alone."

"How do you know?"

"There were two attempts at industrial sabotage

this morning. One involving our computer network, the other involving a prisoner escape from our cell block. It wasn't possible for Diana to be in both places at once. K-Directorate won't rest until they find the other spy."

He stood and joined her in the kitchen. The space was cramped. Sydney knew he was boxing her in. "When K-Directorate suspects you of working against them, they place you before a tribunal. Diana was an exception, tried in absentia. Her sentence was carried out without needing to hear her defense. Do you know why?"

Something caught Sydney's eye—something on the ceiling.

The glow stars.

She hadn't covered the ceiling with them as Francie had, but she had scattered a few throughout the space. Sydney had no doubt that Anna had reported what she'd found in Diana's hand to her superiors. Which meant all Gregoran had to do was glance up.

"Because we knew she was SD-9."

"I don't know what that is," Sydney said.

Gregoran tilted his head and gave her a sarcastic smile. "I doubt that highly. And so does K-Directorate."

"But—but—" Sydney stammered. "You said you knew I was loyal to K-Directorate."

"I said I knew you were loyal to *me*. We've met before, you and I. You know me from a past life." *Josef,* she thought. *He's talking about Josef.*

"There are other forces inside K-Directorate who already have you in their sights. They want you dead, simply as a result of your close ties to Diana." Gregoran's eyes seemed to dance in the low light of the kitchen. Beseeching, they pulled her in. And even though everything he was saying was a lie, Sydney felt herself wanting to believe him.

"I can protect you, Sasha. I *like* you. You're one of my sheep. But you have to come clean with me. You have to tell me everything you know about SD-9 so I can give K-Directorate somebody else to persecute. Otherwise . . ." He placed his forefinger against her temple and mimed pulling the trigger.

Her world swam. In her mind, she heard Sloane's words of advice. *You must maintain your alias.*

And somewhere else, deep in the recesses of her mind, she heard something else. *People will believe any lie. Provided it's big enough.*

It was something Sloane said to her once, after Wilson, her first handler at SD-6, had been exposed as a double agent. Sloane had passed her in the hall and said in a reassuring voice how sorry he was that she had experienced that. Sydney had simply expressed her own confusion. How could she have missed the signs? she had asked. How long had Wilson been working against SD-6 interests right under her nose?

Sloane had put his arm around her. "He fooled me too, Sydney. He fooled all of us. But people will believe any lie. Provided it's big enough."

Sydney looked directly at an expectant Gregoran. She had one recourse: she had to lie. And she had to lie big.

"All right," she whispered. "This is what I can tell you."

14

THE NEXT MORNING, SHE showered and dressed
on autopilot. Her mind was wracked with questions.
What would Gregoran probe for? What angles hadn't
she covered? Her story was good for one thing only:
to buy time. But Gregoran wouldn't be satisfied for
long. He'd investigate her—and her lie—as much as
he could. She was still asking herself those questions
as she held her SD-6 op-tech over the commode,
ready to flush it. But she stopped.

The fingerprint and phone felt like weights in her
hand. Sloane had told her to destroy them both. With
one blow she could smash the phone into pieces and

wash all the vestiges of her life in Los Angeles down the drain.

But you don't have to do that anymore. The cat's out of the bag. Gregoran knows you're a double agent.

That was true. The man who could do her the most harm knew she had her own agenda. If she was going to survive this, who could predict what could come in handy?

* * *

"All right," Sydney had whispered the night before. "This is what I can tell you."

Gregoran drew a satisfied smile, convinced he was about to hear the truth.

"I was recruited by SD-9," Sydney said, "because I could identify you as Josef."

"That's what they want?" he asked. "They're after me?" He seemed to take an absurd delight in being the target of SD-9's attention.

"They did. Encoded in the virus I downloaded—"

"We stopped that upload. It didn't do any damage to our systems."

"Encoded in the virus," she persisted, "was a subvirus. An e-mail that contains two audio files. One was of a speech you gave to Kurtzman-Counter Oil, explaining why K-Directorate would provide security for their overseas investment. The other was a speech from May 1, 1990. A rabble-rousing declaration of revolution, delivered by a quasireligious figure named Josef."

The smile melted from Gregoran's face. "What?" he whispered.

"A cursory examination of the voice prints shows that the two speakers are one and the same," she said as Gregoran darkened. "The subvirus is still on K-Directorate's server."

He reached out and grabbed her roughly. "You're lying," he said through his teeth.

"The e-mail is on a timed release. In forty-eight hours, it will go public."

"To whom?" He laughed. "The media? They'll take no notice and carry on. You've seen too many spy movies, little girl."

"No," Sydney said. "Not to the media. To every active agent inside K-Directorate. I'm sure many people would be fascinated to learn that the man they once hunted is now in charge of their branch."

He shook her roughly, shoving her against the stove. She pinwheeled backward, scrambling for balance. Her hand knocked the teapot off the burning gas jet, and she burned two knuckles on the flame. But she hardly noticed.

Her palm struck out—an instinctive response to

being manhandled—and landed firmly in his solar plexus, sending him staggering backward. "We can fight," she said, her voice brimming with anger, "or you can listen. Because right now, I'm the only one who can stop the virus."

A change came over him. His dark green eyes were shining. His pupils were dilated. It was rage, but there was something else.

She saw the same thing in her sparring matches whenever she faced off against a man. She would land a good head shot or body blow, and this look, the same one Gregoran had, would sweep over their faces. Their moves would be too fast, too uncontrolled after that. Sydney would tell herself to maintain calm after that point, let them lose the round for her. They always did.

She'd asked her instructor about this. He'd smiled and replied, "It masks the fear that they are losing to a woman. A balanced warrior respects the skill, not the sex, of the fighter."

Sydney wasn't sure she believed this until she fought other women. She noticed a disengaged air to their matches. The women's moves were no less deadly than those of her male counterparts, but the women seemed to be saying, *We do this because it's expected by our male superiors. We could talk this out if our bosses would just let us.*

It was fear. Fear shone in Gregoran's eyes as they stood in the kitchen. And at that moment, Sydney knew that Gregoran's hypnotic hold over her had broken.

"You can still stop it?" he asked.

But she wasn't about to reassure him just yet. Her voice didn't waver even though her heart was pounding. "Any attempt to seek out the virus and destroy it results in the e-mail's being sent. The only way to shut it down is by entering the right password. Enter the wrong password and the e-mail will be sent immediately."

She waited, letting him sweat for a few seconds. Then she added, "There were two people who know the right password. You killed one of them this morning."

"Give it to me." He tried to make it sound like an order. But there was no threat, no hint of violence. He sounded as if he was begging.

"Not until I'm safe," she responded.

"What do you want?" he demanded. "Safe passage out of here? I'll give you that. I'll have you on the first plane out of Moscow."

"No," Sydney said. "There's something I have to do first."

* * *

She entered the east wing at K-Directorate and noticed that the guards wouldn't meet her eye. She crossed to her desk with the distinct feeling that people were staring at her, but she couldn't catch anybody in the act.

"Good morning, Ivana," she said as she passed a fellow trainee. Ivana ducked slightly and kept walking without saying hello. *Do they know?* she thought. *Did the lie get out? Did Gregoran talk?* But that couldn't have been the case. It wasn't in Gregoran's interests to reveal he'd been blackmailed by a nineteen-year-old spy. And if he had, she would have been seized at the entrance to the building.

Still, something was going on.

She dropped her purse at her desk and walked into the kitchen. Mina was there, pouring cream into her coffee. When she turned, her eyes grew big at the sight of Sydney. She tried to leave without speaking, but Sydney blocked her.

"What is going on?" Sydney asked.

"Nothing," Mina said. "I have a lot of work to do."

"You don't work," Sydney countered. "You use the cameras to watch your boyfriend all day. Now tell me why I'm being frozen out."

Mina glanced around, pulling Sydney farther into the kitchen. "Look, I can't be seen talking to you, all right?"

"Why not?"

Mina glared at her as if Sydney had just won the

Miss Ditz pageant for the third year in a row. "Because I don't want to be associated with the hussy who had the director of operations in her apartment yesterday."

Sydney wondered how the word had gotten around. But, like all gossips, once Mina started, she couldn't stop.

"Sokolov told everybody. I didn't believe it, of course. Until this morning," Mina said. "Order straight from Gregoran. Hands off Petrova. No investigation. No surveillance. For God's sake, our boss was killed yesterday and suddenly you're in the clear? There's only one way to avoid that kind of scrutiny, Sasha."

"I'm not sleeping with him," Sydney whispered hotly, not sure if rumors to that effect would be good or bad.

Mina put her hands over her ears. "I don't care, I'm not listening. We're not even having this conversation. But if I were you, I'd grow eyes in the back of my head."

"Why?"

Mina mumbled something, dodged past Sydney's arm, and hurried down the corridor. Sydney heard somebody approach her from behind, and she knew who it was before she turned around. The heavy boot steps. The jangling of metal fasteners over a holstered gun.

She turned to stare into the eyes of an enraged

Anna Espinosa. Most women had a detached gaze when they sparred . . . but not all of them.

"Anna, I—"

Anna backhanded Sydney before she could finish the sentence, her wrist connecting with Sydney's jaw in a clean, fierce move. Sydney took two steps back, completely unprepared. The explosion of pain started in her mouth and quickly spread over her face. Her body bent at the waist and she caught hold of the table that extended from the corner of the room. She had taken harder hits before. The surprise of being caught off guard stung more than anything. That, and the fact that she couldn't hit back.

All of K-Directorate, with the exception of Gregoran, thinks you're a surveillance tech, she said to herself. *If you engage here, they'll know you're the other SD-9 mole.*

Anna moved forward and slid the door to the kitchen shut. "Let's have a talk," she said, "you and I." Anna reached down and grabbed Sydney's jaw. She squeezed, and Sydney felt another wave of pain all the way to her spine. Every nerve ending felt on fire. She saw white spots behind her eyes.

"Pietr Gregoran," Anna said, "is off-limits. You don't talk to him. You don't look at him. You don't breathe his air. He's *mine*." Sydney's hands flew over Anna's, wrestling for release. But Anna's grip was unwavering. "If I ever find out you've had additional contact with him, I'll make sure you disappear."

Sydney finally peeled Anna's fingers off her face. She staggered away while Anna stopped to pick up a paper towel. She methodically wiped each finger, as if Sydney were dirty. "And remember," Anna snorted, "I'm Spetsnaz. No one will question your disappearance. No one will even *notice*."

Anna threw the paper towel in the trash and opened the sliding door. "I'm glad," she said over her shoulder, "we had this chance to talk."

Gregoran had told Sydney the night before that she had to tell him everything she knew about SD-9, so that he could give K-Directorate somebody besides Sydney to persecute.

Sydney had an idea who that somebody else could be.

* * *

Leo looked at her when she entered his lab. "Can I help you?" he asked. He had absolutely no idea who she was since she had drugged him the day before.

"My name's Sasha," she said. "Sasha Petrova. I was told you might be able to help me. My jaw got a little close to Anna Espinosa's fist." She leaned in, showing the already swelling bruise that would turn into a bright blue in a few hours.

Leo sucked in sharply, sympathizing. "Yes, yes. This happens all the time." He walked over to a closet and began rummaging around. "Are you allergic to morphine?"

"No." The mannequins with the skin dye were a few feet away. Her eyes scanned the array of models, searching for the coloring that was closest to Anna's.

Leo emerged with a small vial and a hypodermic needle before Sydney could make her move. "Good," he said. "This is a nonaddictive synthetic, so it shouldn't give you any problems." He pulled out a chair for her.

"Kinda crazy what happened yesterday, huh?" she asked, testing the waters.

He dabbed her cheek with an alcohol-dabbed cotton swab. "I suppose," he replied. "I slept through most of it."

"You *slept* through it?"

"Whoever tried to download the virus knocked me out. It was . . ." He paused, still trying to recover the memories he lost. "It was very embarrassing." He drew the liquid into the vial. "Anyway, they already gave me a lie detector test to make sure I wasn't part of it. As if I would ever do something to hurt K-Directorate."

Except you did, Sydney thought. *You just don't remember.* The moment before he plunged the needle in, he added, "They're going through the office now. Everyone else will have to take the test in twenty-four hours."

He gave her the shot. Her cheek screamed in pain again, but the pain was replaced just as quickly with a tingly numbness that called up a memory of the dentist's office.

Twenty-four hours. In twenty-four hours, they'll have me on Leo's lie detector test. And they'll know what I did. If it's as good as Leo says it is, there's no way for me to beat it. I have to move. I have to move tonight.

"Do you have anything for tonight? To help me sleep?" She just needed him to disappear one more time and she'd grab the skin dye she needed.

"Yeah, hang on." He turned his back and she reached out quickly. In two steps she had the small bottle in her hand.

He stopped, staring at the needle in his hand. She noticed and immediately slipped back into her seat. Turning, still staring at the needle, he asked, "Have we met before?'

"Excuse me?"

"You and I? We . . . know each other, don't we?"

"I don't think so."

His eyes went to the needle in his hand, then back to her. A memory stuck somewhere in his brain began to dislodge, as if he were beginning to recall that sometime not too long ago, their positions had been reversed. And Sydney had been the one with the needle.

"Leo?" she asked, trying to keep him from putting the pieces together.

"I never told you my name," he said.

"I heard it in the office," she lied. "Mina was the one who told me to come see you."

"Mina? I don't know a Mina."

She wanted to tell him everything. She wanted to tell him that they were on the same side. That she had done what she had to do to save his life. But she couldn't. Cameras were watching.

"Well, she knows you." Sydney tried to sound upbeat, but she came off as desperate. She felt guilty. "Thanks for your help. I feel much better." All she wanted was to get out of his lab as quickly as possible.

"Don't mention it." He threw the needle in the trash. His eyes never left Sydney as she walked out the door.

She marched across the office, weighing her limited options. On the one hand, she had a mission to complete. On the other, K-Directorate was searching for evidence that she was Diana's partner. Within a day, they would have her attached to a lie detector, and that would be all the proof they needed.

She had to move up the timetable. She had to do something drastic. And she had to hope Anna never found out about it.

She entered Gregoran's office, startling the director, who was talking on a headset connected to his phone. She remembered what Diana had said about owning a room.

Start by making him notice you.

She rested her weight on her right foot and her right hand on her waist. The message to Gregoran was clear: *I have something to talk to you about, and it's more important than whatever work you're doing.* Diana, she hoped, was proud.

Then you make him work for you.

Gregoran let his eyes linger on her as he took his sweet time getting off the phone. Once he finally did, he asked, "Can I help you?"

"Let's have dinner," Sydney announced. "Tonight. I'll give you something that you want."

He considered her words. "Why not now?"

"Tonight," she repeated. "And I pick the place."

"All right. Where?"

She crooked her finger, enticing him forward so that their faces almost met. And then, mindful of the microphones and bugs she knew he had in his office, she whispered the request in his ear.

15

SYDNEY COULDN'T STAY INSIDE the building. That much was obvious.

Somebody had to have seen her go into Gregoran's office. And that somebody would tell somebody else, until eventually word would get back Anna. So when Sydney went up the elevator and out the lobby to Comcor, she was surprised to see a limousine sitting at the curb. Probably some K-Directorate VIP, she told herself. But she was unprepared for the middle-aged man who stepped out and said, "Ms. Petrova?"

She stopped. "Yes?"

"My name is Nikolai. I'm one of Mr. Gregoran's assistants."

She stared at him blankly, waiting for him to offer more.

"Mr. Gregoran asked me to help you prepare for tonight."

"Prepare?" she asked.

"The restaurant you proposed has certain dress requirements," Nikolai said. "Mr. Gregoran was concerned you might not be able to meet them." He beckoned with his hand, as if to imply they didn't have all day.

She climbed into the limousine, overwhelmed. The car felt like the interior of a spaceship. Soft lighting swept over the plush leather. Opposite her was a small bar, above which several television monitors were set in recessed panels. Nikolai entered after her and slammed the door. The car pulled forward.

Nikolai got on his cell phone and began dialing. "What are your measurements?"

"Excuse me?"

"Your clothing. What are you, a size sixteen?"

Sydney blinked. *European sizes are larger.* "Uh, yeah. A sixteen."

Limousine sightings in Los Angeles were nothing compared to the ones in Moscow. Crowds formed around them at stoplights. Sydney heard them debate whether the president or a member of Parliament was inside. A small child leaned forward and pressed his face up against the glass, trying to see inside. He knocked twice. Sydney knocked back. The child jumped back, startled, then squealed with delight.

"Don't do that, please." Until now, Nikolai had been barking orders into his cell phone. "We try not to encourage the rabble."

The limousine pulled up to a combination clothing boutique and spa. Nikolai led her inside. A team of six women waited for her. One approached so quickly, Sydney almost went into a defensive posture. Instead of attacking her, though, the woman flung Sydney's arms up and measured her bust.

The woman promptly burst into tears. "You said she was a four. She's a four and a half!" One of the other women let her head drop in her hands. Nikolai simply turned to Sydney, pointed.

"I'm sorry," Sydney stammered. "I thought I was—"

"I can't have this done by eight o'clock," the woman said to Nikolai.

"Mr. Gregoran asked for the best," Nikolai said. "And you will provide it for him. Anything less is unacceptable." He addressed all of the women. "You have five hours and fifty-six minutes left, starting . . ." He looked at his watch. ". . . now."

The women grabbed Sydney and raced her to an

enormous dressing room. Partitions gave Sydney the space she needed for privacy while staff rushed in and out.

The first outfit they gave her was a dazzling pink. She stepped out from behind a partition to discover that Nikolai was still there. He continued to talk into his cell phone but stopped pacing long enough to look her up and down.

He shook his head.

The women pushed Sydney back behind the partition. "Take it off, take it off!" they screeched. Sydney quickly tore off the dress while they handed her another, this one a royal blue.

She modeled for Nikolai again. "No."

A third dress, this one a black number with lacing that tied tightly in the back like a corset. "Suck in, suck in, suck in," one of the women ordered. Sydney took a deep breath in while they laced up the back of the dress, and felt her lung capacity cut in half while her bust grew a size.

She was about to go in front of Nikolai again when the head woman stopped her. "*Sell* this one," she ordered, and suddenly Sydney felt it was her fault the two previous dresses hadn't worked. But she also knew they were under the gun, so she nodded and exited from behind the partition with a slight strut. She

crossed the room like a runway model, making sure
Nikolai saw the dress from every angle.

"Good. Let's move on."

A small shriek of relief went up among the
women. Nikolai turned and exited the room as
the women untied Sydney. Without giving her so much
as a robe, they dragged her into an overlit yellow room
and slammed her into a reclining salon chair.

"What happened to your *face*?" one of them
exclaimed.

"It's a long story." Sydney sighed.

"Can we cover it up?" another asked.

"Sure, but what about the swelling?'

"Anybody have a cold steak?"

"I have half a lamb sandwich leftover from lunch."

"I don't think lamb will work."

"Just cake on the cover-up," the head woman
snapped. "We don't have time for perfection. This is
beauty triage."

After she showered, they finally gave her a
terrycloth robe and the painful work really began.
Two women attacked her hair, painfully straightening
what was curled. Another worked on her face, pluck-
ing brows and trying different makeup on her. And
another worked solely on her nails.

As the women debated which eye shadow would

work best with the dress, Sydney piped up, "The gray picks up my eyes." All the dressers stopped and stared at her. Sydney smiled apologetically. "I mean, whatever you think is best."

The speed beauty treatment finished, Sydney got laced back into the dress and had her feet shoved into high-heeled shoes. The whole process left her feeling oddly drained. It must have shown, because the head woman marched over and took Sydney's face in her hands, not noticing Sydney wince in pain as she did so.

"Listen to me," she snapped. "I don't care if you're tired. I don't care if you want to go home. You're going to go out there and you're going to look incredible. You know why?"

Sydney wasn't sure what the right response was to this drill-instructor-meets-football-coach speech. "Because you helped me get here?" she ventured.

"That's *right*!" the woman said. She motioned for two of the women, who brought a full-length mirror over to Sydney.

Sydney saw herself in the mirror. She couldn't believe it.

Staring back at her was a statuesque vision. A woman possessed of so much confidence, poise, and strength, she radiated beauty. Sydney unselfconsciously straightened her posture and felt a burst of power surge through her.

I'm going to kick butt, she thought.

"Damn right you are," the lead dresser said, admiring her own handiwork. Startled, Sydney realized she had thought out loud.

I hope I at least said it in Russian.

*   *   *

"I don't understand why you insisted on the purse," Nikolai said tartly in the limousine as they drove to the restaurant. But Sydney needed a place to hide her SD-6 op-tech. And not even the wailing and gnashing of teeth from the dressers could persuade her otherwise.

"So what do you do as Gregoran's assistant?" she asked.

"Whatever he desires," Nikolai said, staring out the window.

"What's he like?" She was hoping he could give her pointers on how to manipulate him.

"I've never met him. He gives me instruction over the phone." Sydney could tell by the disgusted tone in his voice that Nikolai was offended by the lack of courtesy.

"And those instructions are . . ."

"Arranging dates with women such as yourself." Nikolai nodded at her. "Ensuring that the correct bottle of champagne is on ice at his house, that the impressive first editions are on the shelf. Providing what Mr. Gregoran calls the finer things in life."

"And do you get paid well for this sort of job?"

Nikolai shot her a leveling gaze. "Of course not."

Sydney glanced around. "What time is it?"

"Eight-fifty. You'll be there five minutes early, waiting for Mr. Gregoran to arrive."

Sydney rapped on the driver's window. "Turn around."

"What?"

Sydney ignored him. "Drive around the block."

"You'll do no such thing," Nikolai instructed the driver.

Sydney turned to Nikolai, eyes blazing. "Your job is to make this night perfect, right?"

"It is. And I will not ruin it with your parlor games."

"Haven't you ever had a perfect evening that started with your date being late?"

Nikolai fell silent.

"Mr. Gregoran will *wait* for *me,*" Sydney said, then added with a wicked smile, "if he knows what's good for him."

Nikolai caught the driver's eye. "Circle the block."

The restaurant Sydney had picked was an Italian place called Micelli's, which, despite its lush decor

and a top-notch waitstaff, was renowned only for how
bad the food was.

She hadn't picked it for the food anyway but for
the clientele. In addition to K-Directorate, five Mafias
ruled Moscow. They fought over turf like wild dogs,
but Micelli's was neutral ground, where the different
heads could meet to sort out differences, discuss
mergers or simply sit for a meal without risk of ha-
rassment.

Initially all this had happened without the owner's
understanding. He had simply been delighted that a
new, upscale clientele was flooding his small, earnest
business with much-needed cash. But once he was
clued in to the identities of his patrons, he had faced
an unpleasant choice: close the business and start
over, or let the heads of the families use his establish-
ment as a meeting place. Addicted to success in an
impossible economy, he had chosen the latter.

But rather than pouring money into preparing
better food, he had became paranoid about police or
other surveillance organizations like K-Directorate
bugging his restaurant. So he had begun to sink his
profits into sensitive bug-sweeping technology. Ironi-
cally, this only fostered a greater sense of security in
the Mafia families. Micelli's became a safe house of
sorts for them. And rather than target it as a place to

make arrests, the police decided that it was safer to let it stand. The restaurant became a demilitarized zone in an ongoing fight, a place where law enforcement could sit down with criminals to talk them out of gang wars that were killing hundreds of innocents.

So based on her knowledge of the Russian elite, Sydney picked Micelli's. Gregoran wouldn't be wired, because if he was, alarms would go off like a test of the Emergency Broadcast System the moment he walked in the door. And Anna's Spetsnaz team wouldn't be able to grab Sydney while she was there—not without a dozen guns being drawn the moment five paramilitary officers entered the restaurant.

She assumed that Gregoran knew all this too, and even appreciated her choice. After all, he had as much to gain from the privacy as she did.

* * *

At 9:10, the limousine pulled up to Micelli's. Sydney could see Gregoran waiting inside, checking his watch.

She turned to Nikolai. She didn't like this man, but she respected him in an odd way. Like Leo, he was a man struggling to survive under the hard gaze of K-Directorate. "Thank you," she said. And she meant it.

Nikolai rolled his eyes. "You're the one who has to go on the date with him."

Sydney opened the door to the limousine and hit the pavement with both feet. When she rose out of the car gracefully, she half expected flashbulbs to pop. With confident, purposeful strides, she made it from the car to the restaurant in three steps. Somebody opened the door for her.

The maitre d' took one look at her and said, "Right this way, madame." Sydney followed him through the restaurant to Gregoran's table. Along the way, she heard a hum fill the restaurant. She was at the center of it.

Still, she stayed behind the maitre d' so that Gregoran wouldn't see her. He looked up as the maitre d' presented her and pulled out her chair. In silent amazement, he studied her as she sat, while another server placed her napkin in her lap for her and a third poured a glass of wine that Gregoran had already ordered.

Once Gregoran and Sydney were alone, Gregoran said nothing. He simply drank her in. Sydney let him. She had all the power. And she knew it.

"Like a dream she appears," he finally murmured.

There were no menus. The waiter listed the evening's selections. Once he had departed, Gregoran asked, "May I have the password?"

"After dinner, Pietr." It was the first time she'd used his first name. He frowned but let it go.

"Your plan was actually quite ingenious," he said.

"I asked Leo to perform a search of all known viruses in the system. Do you know what he told me?"

Sydney folded her hands in her lap, tightly. He was testing her, probing her. How much did she really know about computer networks? How well she responded would determine whether he would continue to buy her lie.

"The human body has roughly two dozen communicable viruses inside it at any given time," she replied. "We don't notice because our immune system is constantly fighting them. A network like K-Directorate is no different. The price you pay for instant data transfer—e-mails, file downloads, what have you—is that a small percentage of the data will be corrupt. You can't clean all the viruses out of your computer network. It would drain your resources. Besides, most of those viruses are relatively benign." She took a sip of water, hoping he wouldn't notice her hand was shaking. "If I had to guess, I'd say Leo found between three and four hundred."

"A-plus," he said. "Would you mind at least giving me the name of the virus? I mean, I should know that, shouldn't I, if I want to clean out what you laid in there?"

"The e-mail is wrapped in your autoexec.bat file." She knew from a cursory SD-6 briefing on computer systems that plenty of viruses lodged themselves there. "The name is unimportant. When you log on to the system tomorrow, enter the password I give you instead of your own. That will direct the virus to destroy itself."

Gregoran scowled and shook his head. "Leo seemed awfully interested in what I was looking for. I would have thought the two of you were in league together if we hadn't found him passed out in his own lab yesterday."

She could only assume Leo was acting this way because of his newly recovered memories. "He had nothing to do with this," she said sharply.

He glanced up at her tone, amused. "Really."

The last thing she needed was to have Gregoran's attention distracted from her. She'd already lost Diana that way. "Why is the network still down?" she asked. "I thought you'd be back online today."

"That was an executive order," Gregoran replied. "From me. I didn't want some IS fool snooping around and messing with your virus accidentally."

"So everybody's still locked out?"

"Not everybody," he replied. "The inner committee still have their privileges. As do I."

Meaning he could get online. His computer could download the virus. Her plan could work.

But to do it, she'd need to bypass the biometric sensor on his mouse.

She needed his fingerprint.

Sydney scooted over to the seat adjacent to Pietr's. He was obviously surprised. But she pretended to be preoccupied with bringing her purse to her lap. She leaned over and cooed, "We're not going to talk shop all night, are we?"

"That depends," he replied. "What would you like to talk about?"

"How did a rabble-rouser like you end up working in a corporate environment like K-Directorate? That would strike me as the last place you'd want to be."

"A woman recruited me," he answered. "She was a major in the KGB."

"I didn't know women were allowed to reach that rank."

"They're not. She was an exception. She was . . . magnificent."

She rested her chin on one hand. *Keep him talking,* she thought.

"What was so amazing about her?"

"She was one of the founding members of K-Directorate when we decided to go underground. Or rather, officially underground." Sydney's right hand searched for the fingerprint in her purse. There was her phone. . . . There was her lipstick. . . . "She had bigger goals than any other members of the Duma. She wanted to unite all five Mafia organizations. Bring them under one roof.

"She could have done it too. She had the force of personality. She had the vision. But she got distracted."

"By what?" Sydney kept her face bright, but secretly she despaired. Her hand had felt every item in her purse, but she hadn't found the fingerprint. Carefully she started over, this time from the top.

"An obsession," he told her. "Over some philosopher's antiquities. She was convinced if she could put together all the pieces of some treasure hunt, she would . . ." He waved it away, as if too disappointed to go on. Instead, he turned and looked at her. "You know, you kind of remind me of her."

The fingerprint, which had meshed into the lining of her purse, lifted at the moment into her searching hand. With her thumb and index finger, she removed the adhesive backing. The print lifted effortlessly to her finger.

"That's sweet," she smiled. "I think."

She dropped the purse from her lap and kicked it under the table.

"Do you know what my father always said?" she asked. "'Judge a man by his hands.'" Gregoran looked at his, almost playfully. "'If they're worn, dirty, or blistered,' " she explained, " 'then you know he's a hard worker.' To which my mother added, 'And you know he's not cheating on you.' "

She reached over and took Gregoran's hand. "What do your hands say about you, Pietr?"

They were smooth and soft, like a baby's. "I don't think I'd meet your father's criteria." He grinned.

She placed her hand flat against his and pressed lightly. She had no idea whether she was getting the imprint she needed. She also wasn't sure she could hold it there for eight seconds, as Graham had directed.

"Maybe not," she said, moving even closer to him, letting her eyes dazzle him. "But you have nice hands. A woman notices these things."

"Really?" He tried to pull away. She quickly wrapped her other hand around his, locking it in place. She kept him in her orbit by giving him her most seductive look. Her mind said, *If he doesn't burst into laughter, I might.* But the look had its intended effect. He stayed in her grasp.

"Oh yes." She smiled. "I'm surprised Agent Espinosa didn't comment on it when the two of you were dating."

Gregoran sat back, yanking his hand away. "Agent Espinosa"—he sighed— "has delusions about our relationship."

"Well, those delusions nearly gave me a broken jaw."

"I'll talk to her," he grumbled.

"Don't," Sydney insisted. "It will only make things worse. Trust me on that."

Gregoran stared at her as the appetizers arrived. "How do I know you're not going to sell me out the first chance you get?"

"A lot of people put their faith in you, Josef. Now you're going to have to put your faith in *me*."

* * *

He dropped her off at the door of her flat. "All right," he said. "Enough games. What is the password?"

"*Demetria*."

"Yes. It's the name of a friend of mine. But don't jump the gun and try to destroy the virus tonight, the system will record your login. The guards will notice you. It'll be that much more difficult to extract you. Wait until tomorrow morning. Do it as part of your normal daily routine."

He nodded. *Either he really thinks I'm taking him with me,* Sydney mused, *or he's the best actor in the world.*

"There's one more thing," he said.

"What?"

Gregoran lunged forward and kissed her. Sydney didn't fight it. She had sold him too many lies to stop him.

The fact was, he wasn't a bad kisser. But she felt nothing. No sparks. No chemistry. When she kissed Noah, her heart sang. With Gregoran, the only interesting thing about the kiss was how dull it was.

He broke it off and let his forehead rest against hers. "I've been wanting to do that since I met you," he whispered.

"Go home," she whispered back, pushing him away.

Smiling, he returned to his limousine. She watched him go, waiting until the taillights disappeared before she felt it was safe to move.

But on her first step back toward her building, she was caught in a wash of headlights. A car screeched forward out of a dark alley, heading straight toward her.

Her mind short-circuited—it was a mad, bizarre threat that she barely had time to process. She dove out of the way at the last possible second. There was no timing or grace to it. All she could think was *There's a car. There's a car coming at me. There's a car coming at me and it's going to run me over! Jump! Jump! Jump!*

The car swerved, trying to sideswipe her. But it missed completely and fishtailed out of control. The door swung open and Anna—still dressed in fatigues—staggered out.

"I told you to leave Pietr alone!" she screamed.

That was when Sydney saw the gun in her hand.

16

SYDNEY PULLED OFF HER high heels and moved toward Anna. She could tell that Anna was drunk, and hoped that meant that her aim would be shaky.

Dive! Sydney dove to the ground as a bullet flew through the air, then scrambled toward her attacker, pulling Anna to the ground before she could fire

Where's the gun? Where's the gun? Sydney thought wildly as Anna somersaulted from her back onto her hands, then executed a perfect back hand-spring onto her feet. She was in a kempo karate stance, a perfect defensive position.

"You," Anna spat, taking in Sydney's Krav Maga skills. "You're the other mole. You were working with that wench, Di—"

Not wanting to let her finish, Sydney went into a scissor kick. As Anna blocked it with her forearms, Sydney countered with a one-handed blow to her abdomen. Anna turned sideways, putting Sydney on the defensive.

I can't win this fight! Sydney thought, panicking. *Not if I keep losing ground.* Her dress was making Krav Maga moves nearly impossible, and Anna, her rage fueled by both adrenaline and alcohol, was a double threat.

Sydney landed two quick rabbit punches to the sternum and jaw—and to her consternation, Anna smiled as blood trickled over her teeth.

"I sent your surveillance unit home," Anna said. "I didn't want any witnesses. But now?" Anna spat on the ground. "I would appreciate an audience."

She came at Sydney with an open-palmed slice to the bridge of her nose. As Sydney went to block it, Anna grabbed her wrist.

"Ow!" *You've got to get out of this. She's going to snap your wrist like a twig unless you do something. . . .*

Sydney head-butted her opponent, sending waves of pain through her own skull. But at least she'd bought a moment to think. Blood was pouring from Anna's nose.

As Sydney had hoped, Anna's hands flew from Sydney's wrist to her own nose.

You may get out of this yet, Bristow.

Sydney's first instinct was to finish her now, before she had a chance to recover. But then she remembered her purse. She had dropped it when Anna had sideswiped her. And inside the purse were her phone, Gregoran's lifted fingerprint, and the skin dye she'd stolen from the lab.

Sydney's plan was to disguise herself as Anna and get inside K-Directorate. But it would take more than just a darker complexion. She would need Anna's clothes, her gun, her hair. . . .

Suddenly Anna ran back toward her car.

She's going for her gun! Sydney grabbed her purse and made it inside her apartment.

Bang!

Sydney raced up the stairs, feeling splintered wood under her bare, bleeding feet.

A door behind her opened. Anna had lied! A member of the surveillance detail had stayed behind—

But no. It was Mrs. Andropov, staring at Sydney with frightened eyes.

"Stay inside, please," Sydney begged, unlocking her own door and slamming it behind her. This door, with its rusted hinges, was like tissue paper to Anna. But that was okay. Sydney just needed a head start.

All she had was sixty seconds. Maybe less.

She started in her bedroom, quickly slipping her bloody feet into a pair of loafers, then swept the sheets off the bed. She wrapped her fists in them and moved through the apartment, smashing the light fixtures and collecting glass in the cloth as she went. She spread the glass on the floor until there was a trail of it from the doorway.

She quickly ripped the cheap cloth to small pieces, then set the pieces aside and grabbed the broom that had been shoved between the refrigerator and the stove by the previous occupant. She leaned it on the stove and used karate to break the straw head cleanly from the handle in one blow. She then took the three-foot long staff in her hand. It wasn't perfect, but it would have to do.

She crouched in the dark. And she waited.

Judging by the sound coming from the door, Sydney knew Anna had just removed one of the hinges. She turned to see the door hanging precariously from its remaining hinge, as if deciding which way it wanted to fall. Then, with a nudge from Anna, it slammed into the apartment. The muscles in Sydney's legs screamed at her to fly forward, to strike. But Sydney couldn't give up her position without isolating Anna's next move.

She pushed the door in to draw fire. She wants to see if I'm armed.

Anna's hand snaked into the apartment, feeling around for the light switch. She found it, flipped the switch, then pulled her hand back when she discovered the lights had been killed.

Now she knows I've laid a trap for her. She's going to move in three . . . two . . . one . . .

Anna dove through the door, rolling into the apartment—and onto the glass. Her heavy clothing protected her, but she immediately realized her disadvantage when she stood and her boots crunched on the shards. Her first instinct would be to find a less dangerous surface to fight on.

Sydney gave her legs the relief they'd been begging for and flew forward. Her knees popped as she approached Anna in a half crouch. Anna sensed the movement, but she was uncertain as she tried to find solid footing. She also wasn't prepared for the short staff Sydney was wielding.

Sydney's first hit with the broomstick landed squarely on Anna's spine. Anna took the full brunt of it, and the blow was so clean that Sydney felt the staff bounce off her vertebrae. The vibrations rippled up the broomstick and hummed in Sydney's fingers.

Sydney moved with the rebound, twirling away from Anna and dropping to one knee. The length of the staff allowed her to stay off the broken glass, and her second shot landed squarely on Anna's knee. Sydney thought she heard the sound of bone chipping beneath the howl of pain from her opponent. Now Anna was on the floor. She swung at Sydney in sheer rage, but without strength or aim. Sydney dodged the blow easily.

The fight's over now. She just doesn't realize it.

Sydney jumped to the balls of her feet, bobbing and weaving. She swung the staff once, twice, three times, hitting Anna at sensitive points on her neck.

There was no more yelling, no more thrashing. Anna knew what Sydney had done, and she knew she was beaten. Seconds later, she fell to the floor and began to shake violently, in the throes of a grand mal seizure.

The staff slipped from Sydney's fingers, serving no further purpose. She grabbed the torn bed sheets, intending to tie Anna up once the spasms gave way to an unconscious paralysis. Anna breathed in short gasps as Sydney loomed over her. But her focus wasn't on Sydney. It was on the ceiling.

"The stars . . . ," Anna whispered. And then she passed out.

Sydney rolled Anna over and began to bind her hands behind her back. A scream from the hallway stopped her. Sydney looked up to see of the horrified face of Mrs. Andropov.

"I knew you were a strange duck," her next-door neighbor yelped. "I knew it the moment you walked in!"

"Mrs. Andropov, please—" Sydney said.

"I'm calling the police!" But for a moment, the woman didn't move. She seemed hypnotized by the strange sight of her neighbor tying up another woman.

Sydney's eyes fell to Anna's hands. "Mrs. Andropov, look!" She unbound Anna and held up her right hand.

Mrs. Andropov had turned to leave, but she looked back to see what Sydney was showing her, and she froze.

It was Anna's Spetsnaz ring.

Slowly Mrs. Andropov approached the figure on the floor, as if it were an anaconda that could come to life at any moment and swallow her whole.

Sydney breathed heavily, her heart pounding as she watched Mrs. Andropov try to make sense of what she was seeing.

This was what Sydney had always truly feared. Not risking her own life—her skills and intelligence would either get her out of a jam or they wouldn't. But putting her faith in someone else, someone who had no reason to trust or believe her—*that* was terrifying.

"What do you need from me, dear?" Mrs. Andropov said quietly.

Relief washed over Sydney. She looked from Mrs. Andropov to Anna, then back to Mrs. Andropov.

"Do you still have that curling iron?" she asked.

17

KILLING PEOPLE FOR K-DIRECTORATE paid well.

Sydney and Mrs. Andropov had a hard time carrying Anna to her house, which was in one of the city's wealthiest neighborhoods. But a private residence, as opposed to an apartment building, meant no security to worry about, no nosy neighbors. Sydney had found Anna's address on the driver's license in her wallet and had driven the car while Mrs. Andropov followed.

"Ach, what does this girl eat?" Mrs. Andropov

asked as they carried her up the steps to her front door.

"Don't worry about it," Sydney said, pulling Anna's keys out of her pocket and unlocking the door. "Just keep her head elevated."

They carried her inside and dumped her on the couch in the living room of the one-story house. The decor was spare but elegant. Overall, the place reminded Sydney of a showroom—it was nice, but she'd never want to live in it. It had a cold, unfeeling touch.

Still, Mrs. Andropov whistled as she took it all in. "Nice place," she mumbled.

Sydney moved to the bedroom, where Anna's closets were filled with K-Directorate black fatigues. She took off the elegant dress Nikolai had picked out for her and pulled on the paramilitary outfit. The clothes were two sizes too big for Sydney's slender form, so she rolled up the sleeves and tucked the pant legs into the enormous boots that swamped her feet.

She retreated into the bathroom and pulled out the skin dye she'd taken from Leo's lab. When mixed with water, the tone formed a rich base that Sydney was able to apply to her face, her hands, and her arms up to her elbow. She gauged her progress against pictures of Anna. The pictures, like the entire house, seemed impersonal. In each, Anna's smile was plastered on in an unpleasant expression she obviously wasn't used to.

"How do I look?" Sydney asked when she emerged.

Mrs. Andropov let out a small scream. She covered her face with her hands. "Good," she murmured. Peering out from behind her fingers, she said, "Too good."

As Sydney bent over Anna and pulled some hairs from her head, Mrs. Andropov made a grumbling noise.

"I want to take something," the woman said with a pout. "They took my Gregor—what do I get?"

Sydney grabbed the ring off Anna's finger. "Here. Take this."

Mrs. Andropov scowled as she took it. "Why would I want this?"

Sydney smiled as she unclipped Anna's ID with her gloved hand. "Trust me. Anna's going to rue the day she lost it."

* * *

Mrs. Andropov dropped Sydney off three blocks from the Comcor entrance. Sydney pulled her cap down over her head as she got out of the car. "You remember the plan?" she asked the older woman.

Mrs. Andropov nodded. "Go home and clean up your apartment. Be back here in ninety minutes to pick you up."

"And if I'm not here?"

"I don't even slow down," Mrs. Andropov answered. "I circle the block and go home to bed."

Sydney hesitated. She was placing a lot of trust in a lonely woman who had no reason to do any of this.

Suddenly Mrs. Andropov fell into a fit of giggles. "What's so funny?" Sydney asked, alarmed. Had the tension made this woman snap?

"Nothing. I just feel like a spy, that's all." Sydney smiled, relieved. Mrs. Andropov looked like the woman in her wedding picture again. She was ready to take on the world—this time without her husband.

No, Sydney corrected herself, *she's doing this for her husband.* She tipped her hat and slammed the door.

Sydney dug out her cell phone as she began the walk to K-Directorate. After the third ring, a sleepy voice picked up. "Hello?"

"It's Sasha."

She heard him breathing. "Who?" he demanded.

"Sasha Petrova, Leo. You also know me as Sydney Bristow."

"Never heard of you."

"Do you still want to get out of K-Directorate?"

"Who is this? Is that a joke?"

"Think, Leo, think. You thought we'd met before. You were right. I was the one who didn't like broccoli, remember?"

There was an agonizing pause. "You're the . . . You work for SD-6?"

Relief flooded her. "Yes." She'd counted on this. Graham had said that anything smaller than a rhino would be knocked out by the drugs in that pen. Leo wasn't rhino-sized, but he was bigger than the average male. Meaning he would have metabolized the drugs differently than Graham had. His memory wipe wouldn't be complete, which was why, when he had seen her the next day, he'd had a vague recollection of who she was.

"I can get you out of K-Directorate. That's what you want, right? You're tired of making new and efficient ways of killing people. You're tired of people like Gregoran profiting off you. Leo, I can extract you. But I need one small favor." And she told him what it was.

"I can't do that," Leo said.

Sydney was twenty feet away from the entrance to Comcor.

"Then I'm dead. And you'll be at K-Directorate forever. Two-twelve, Leo. Remember that." She paused.

"I'm counting on you," she whispered. And then she hung up.

She stared at the entrance to K-Directorate. All of her training over the past year and all of the advice she'd received over the past four days came swirling together.

She slid Anna's ID in the key card reader at the glass doors and saw Anna's name and face appear on the security monitor inside. The guards inside frantically put out the cigarettes they were smoking and buzzed her in.

You are Anna Espinosa, she thought, throwing back her shoulders. *Go in there and take it.*

She strode in, letting her uniform radiate authority. The guards stood at attention and saluted her as she walked by. They didn't even make eye contact.

She pressed the down button and the elevator opened. She caught her reflection in the shiny metal of the closing doors. With a Spetsnaz hat pulled low over her made-up face and her quickly curled hair, she barely resembled herself. From just under the brim of her hat, her eyes flitted up to the camera in one corner of the ceiling.

They see you. They know you're here. Don't do anything stupid. Don't panic. Don't run. Go about your business like you have every right to be here.

The doors opened and Sydney walked through the oppressively dark wing, her footsteps echoing in the space. At Gregoran's door, she hurriedly went through Anna's key ring. If Gregoran and Anna were having an affair, there was a chance he'd given her a key. If not, Sydney hoped that maybe Anna had secretly had a key made as part of her obsession with him. Either way, Sydney hit the jackpot on the third try.

In the office, Sydney booted up the computer. She still hadn't taken off the fingerprint she'd made when she'd pressed her hand against Gregoran's in the restaurant. She'd been afraid the imprint might be destroyed if she removed it. But that had been one street fight and one breaking-and-entering charge ago. She could only guess what had happened to the print in the interim.

The fingerprint prompt appeared on Gregoran's screen. She placed her finger under the metal sleeve on his mouse.

Please, please, please, she thought. *Please work.*

The computer screen read: SCANNING . . . SCAN-NING . . . SCANNING . . .

Then: ERROR.

Sydney felt her heart stop.

The computer screen flashed: RESCANNING . . . RESCANNING . . . RESCANNING . . .

Finally, it blinked: ID APPROVED. WELCOME, PIETR GREGORAN!

She opened the URL window. The cursor blinked at her. Okay, it asked, where do you want to go?

The URL . . . the URL . . .

What was the URL?

She closed her eyes and let her fingers fly over the keypad on the right side of the keyboard. When she opened them, a window had appeared. It was the SD-6 FTP. The familiar status bar popped up: HYDRA.EXE . . . DOWNLOADING . . .

This time, Sydney promised herself, she wasn't leaving until the transfer was complete.

She grabbed her SD-6 phone and pulled up Graham's preprogrammed number.

She was under seven stories of concrete and wondered whether she would even get a signal. But Graham had once explained to her that SD-6 phones used a passive terahertz wave. They could pass through the densest materials to reach a satellite.

"What are you doing?" Graham screamed into the phone without saying hello. "You can't use this signal! It may have been compromised!"

"That's what I'm counting on," Sydney said. "Can you reprogram the SIM card in this phone with dummy SD-6 numbers?" she asked.

"Yeah," he mumbled, "I guess. What'd you have in mind?"

"A quick frame-up. It doesn't have to be good, just convincing for the moment."

Sydney could hear Graham typing on his computer. "I'll need about three minutes." Sydney looked at the download status. Even though the bar was still going haywire, she was definitely making progress. Three minutes should be perfect.

"I'll call you back, but *don't* pick up," Graham ordered. "I need to get to your voice mailbox in order to reprogram."

"Got it," Sydney said, about to click off.

"Hey, Syd?"

"Yeah?"

"It's good to hear your voice again."

Sydney smiled. She had forgotten that there were people in L.A. who were pulling for her. "I'll see you in thirty-six hours," she promised before hanging up.

She checked her watch. It was 2:13. One minute past the time she had promised Leo. She took a deep breath and did the most difficult thing she'd ever had to do.

She turned and stared straight into the camera in the corner of the office.

Five seconds. She had to do it for five seconds.

They were the longest five seconds of her life.

"Agent Espinosa?" It was a young man's voice. Sydney turned to see a flashlight sweeping under the crack in the door. One of the guards must have been dispatched to investigate. She looked at the computer. The download was 73 percent complete.

She couldn't take this guy; that would only attract more attention. She had to find some other way to distract him.

The guard poked his head into the office to find a huddled, heaving mass bent over Gregoran's desk. "Agent Espinosa . . . ?" he asked again.

Sydney sniffled and lifted her head off the desk. She cradled her forehead in one of her hands. "I can't believe it," she moaned. "Pietr is cheating on me."

The guard hesitated at the door, not sure what the appropriate response was to a heartbroken psychopath. "Agent Espinosa . . . is that you?"

"Yes, it's me, you piece of garbage!" Sydney barked, standing suddenly. "What did they teach you in officer training? Did you forget how to salute a superior officer?" The guard dropped his flashlight in his rush to salute. Sydney wasted no time in scooping it up.

She shined the light in his eyes. The guard winced, squinting both from the glare of the flashlight and his blunder in dropping it. "What's your name, soldier?" Sydney asked in a low growl.

"Officer Egorov, ma'am," the guard replied, his eyes glued to the wall beyond Sydney.

"Tell me, Egorov," Sydney said, advancing on him while continuing to blind him with the light. "Have you ever been cheated on?"

"No—no, ma'am," Egorov stammered.

"Of course not. A boy like you. You're the one who *breaks* their hearts, aren't you?"

A tiny bead of sweat appeared on Egorov's brow. "No, ma'am," he practically yelped. "I mean, I never—"

"I don't know which is worse." Sydney sighed. "The fact that he's sleeping around or that he's doing it with that floozy Petrova."

Egorov was now so thoroughly baffled by this interrogation that all he could say was "Yes, ma'am." *Yes, ma'am. Whatever you say ma'am. Please don't kill me, ma'am.* Sydney practically had the flashlight pressed against his eyeballs. She flipped the light off, the exact effect she had been hoping for: Egorov blinked the spots away from his eyes, trying to alleviate his temporary blindness.

Get out now, she told herself, *while he can't see you.*

Sydney circled back to Gregoran's desk. "You're a valuable contributor to K-Directorate, Egorov,"

Sydney said, covering her movement. "I'll make sure to mention that in your next performance review." She glanced at the computer screen just in time to see the status bar leap from 99.78% to 100%. She shut down the computer before it had a chance to beep at her.

Without breaking her stride, she completed the circle around Egorov and shoved the flashlight into his gut. He fumbled with it, not sure what it was as his eyes continued to adjust.

Sydney was fifty feet away from the elevator when the phone rang in her hand. It was Graham calling to reprogram the cell. She couldn't answer it or turn it off, but holding on to it made her feel like a moving target.

From a pocket she took one of the hairs she'd pulled from Anna's head and shut it in the clasp of the phone. Then she dropped the phone into a trash can, where it continued to ring, muffled.

Egorov locked the office behind her. He noticed the ringing phone and dug it out. Sydney heard the rustling behind her but didn't look back. She was so close to the elevators, she couldn't risk checking on Egorov. Not even after he called out, "Agent Espinosa! Don't you want your phone?"

Sydney hit the elevator button. The elevator hadn't been summoned since she'd gotten off, so the doors opened instantly. She turned to see that Egorov was running toward her now, waving the cell phone. But he stopped, confused, as the doors shut . . .

Sydney counted the seconds as the elevator rose. *Don't panic,* she reminded herself. *And don't run.*

The same guards waited for her at their posts when she stepped off the elevator. "Attention!" she cried. "Superior officer on the floor!" The guards dutifully stood and saluted her.

One of their phone lines lit up. One of them reached to answer it.

"I said," Sydney growled, "stand . . . at . . . *attention*!"

The guard did as he was told. Another line lit up. Followed by a third.

"Agent Espinosa, please," the other guard said. "It's security calling. It's our jobs if we don't answer it."

Sydney unholstered the 9mm from her side. She pointed it at the phone and pulled the trigger. The phone exploded and the guards cowered, trying to dodge white-hot shrapnel and the rage of Anna Espinosa.

"It's your *lives* if you do," Sydney hissed. The guards trembled and resumed their saluting position. Sydney made herself look at them with Anna's intense stare. Finally, she shook her head and headed out. "We need to work on the chain of command around here," she muttered.

And with that, she was out the door.

Three blocks, she thought. *I'll never make it. They'll stop me. They'll track me down and that will be it.*

A car flashed its high beams from a nearby alley.

It was Anna's car.

Dumbfounded, Sydney watched as it pulled out, cut a wide swath around the empty street, and pulled up next to her.

Mrs. Andropov was behind the wheel. She leaned over and opened the door for Sydney. "I know you gave me her ring," she said "But can I also keep her car?"

*   *   *

It had taken Sydney twenty minutes to convince Mrs. Andropov that, no, she couldn't keep the car. It was too big a piece of evidence. And besides, it was damaged. Why would the woman want it?

"Have you seen this?" Mrs. Andropov ran her hand over the interior. "Finest Corinthian leather."

But Sydney got her way.

They traded cars and returned to their building. Sydney quickly changed clothes and scrubbed off the skin dye. Mrs. Andropov had done an excellent job of cleaning her apartment. The light fixtures had all been replaced, the torn sheets replaced by a spare set from Mrs. Andropov's own linen closet, and the blood wiped from the floors. She had even scraped the stars off the ceiling.

Sydney entered Mrs. Andropov's apartment looking like her old self as her neighbor put on a pot of tea. "How much time do we have?" Mrs. Andropov asked.

Sydney looked out the window to see the black van pull up outside her building. "They're already here."

Heavy boots clomped up the stairs and fists pounded on Sydney's apartment door. "Petrova!" they shouted. "Come out with your hands up!"

Sydney and Mrs. Andropov looked at each other. Sydney nodded. This was it.

Mrs. Andropov swung open the door. "Who's making all this fuss at three in the morning?"

The men, led by Sokolov, looked surprised to see Mrs. Andropov's door open, but they followed her inside. They found Sydney cowering on the couch, cup of tea in hand.

"Come with us, Petrova," Sokolov ordered. "You're wanted for questioning."

Sydney rose. Sokolov spun her around and clicked handcuffs on her.

"Leave that poor girl alone!" Mrs. Andropov cried. "She's already been harassed once by you people tonight! She's been in here crying on my shoulder, the dear, scared half to death!"

Sokolov ignored her. "We got you, Petrova. She told us everything. And since it's gonna be Anna's word against yours, who do you think K-Directorate's going to believe?"

They began to march her out of the bedroom. Sokolov leaned in—he couldn't help it. He whispered in her ear, "You're *ours*."

18

HANDCUFFED TO A CHAIR, in the middle of the speaking pit in the auditorium where Diana had been killed, Sydney had a lot of time to think.

She had known from the beginning that Sokolov and the rest of the team would come for her. *When K-Directorate suspects you of working against them,* Gregoran had told her, *they place you before a tribunal.* Since they hadn't killed her yet, she could only assume that was where she was.

In the meantime, she inspected her surroundings. The chair was bolted to the floor, but the bolts appeared new. They moved in their grooves, giving her just enough slack to shift her weight and avoid losing circulation. But there was no relief from the cuffs, and she could only imagine that her wrists had turned purple by now.

She lost all sense of time. The spotlight had blasted her the moment Sokolov and his team had marched her into the auditorium. She could make out the balcony but not enough to tell who might be up there.

After what felt like days but must have been only hours, she heard movement. People. Several people. Sydney couldn't identify the silhouettes, but she assumed it was the inner committee, gathering to hear the case.

They suspected her, naturally. And the thing was, they were right to suspect her. They had every reason to believe that she was Diana's partner because it was the truth.

All she could do was shift the blame. And hope that Leo had come through for her.

Finally, Gregoran entered and stood by her side. He didn't look at her, just turned to face the men in suits who watched from the balcony. He carried himself with an odd formality, and Sydney noticed a bead of sweat on his temple.

"Sasha Petrova," a voice boomed through the auditorium. "You are being held under suspicion of crimes against this intelligence organization. This hearing is an opportunity for you to defend yourself before we render judgment."

Sydney blinked into the light. She bided her time. If she responded too quickly, she would appear overly prepared. Too late and she would obviously be planning her answer.

"What are the charges?" she asked in a meek voice.

"Conspiracy to download materials damaging to K-Directorate."

She took a deep breath, letting it catch in her throat. "Don't I get a lawyer?" she asked. "Isn't that part of our new democratic court system?"

"You signed the waivers," another voice told her "You gave up all due process rights when you agreed to work here. That means we control your fate."

She looked down, willing tears to come. "How can I defend myself," she asked, "when I don't know what I've done?"

"Liar!" Anna's voice rang out. She emerged from the darkness, not in the balcony, but on the ground level. "You know exactly what you've done!" Anna stayed out of the pool of light, not wanting to be tarnished by its implication.

"Pietr?" Sydney begged Gregoran. As if somehow he could save her. Gregoran looked away, shamed.

"Don't address him!" Anna barked. "Tell us what you did last night."

Sydney pretend to gather herself, but the truth was, she had this story down cold.

"I had dinner with Director Gregoran last night—"

"What did you discuss?" the first voice asked.

"What do you talk about on a date? Everything and nothing. Where we come from."

"Director Gregoran, is this true?"

Gregoran looked up at his invisible interrogators. "Yes."

Sydney understood what was going on. Gregoran's computer had been used to downloaded the virus. He was rumored to be seeing Sasha. And he'd called off all surveillance on her to protect his own secrets.

She wasn't the only one on trial here. It was perfect.

"What happened at the conclusion of dinner?" Anna demanded. "You kissed him, didn't you? You discussed plans to sabotage K-Directorate and then you kissed him."

"Yes," Sydney sniffled. "Yes, I kissed him. But then I went home. We didn't talk about any. . . what did you call it? Sabotage?"

"Then what happened?" Voice Number Two called out.

"Then Agent Espinosa tried to kill me."

Mumbling broke out in the balcony. Anna turned to the tribunal. "I was trying to neutralize an enemy spy!"

"She was drunk," Sydney corrected her. "She tried to run me over with her car. She staggered out and said I was trying to steal her man—"

"You were!" Anna said hotly. Then, covering her own personal outburst, she added, "I mean, you were trying to steal him for your cause."

Sydney shook her head. "Agent Espinosa kept saying she would fix it so I would never see Pietr again. She was going to hurt us both. Then she beat me."

"What about me?" Anna exclaimed. "Look at the bruises on my face! I have two broken ribs because of this woman!"

"Agent Espinosa," Sydney said, her eyes wide. "Where is your Spetsnaz ring?"

It was a red herring, a question that had nothing to do with what they were talking about. But it derailed Anna's rant. A Spetsnaz never took off his ring. Never. The fact that Anna had lost it meant she had been careless.

"You came here last night," Anna said, trying to steer the conversation back to what she knew. "You walked in here posing as *me*!"

"That's not true," Sydney protested.

"It is!" Anna screamed. She was well into the light by now, shouting directly into Sydney's face. "It is, you witch, and you know it!"

Sydney faced the tribunal. "If these charges have merit, where's the physical evidence?"

"We're still compiling that," Voice Number One said. "We do, however, have an eyewitness."

This came as a surprise to Anna. She turned as the doors opened and Shostok timidly entered.

"Mr. Egorov," Voice Number One said. "You entered into your log that you caught an intruder in Director Gregoran's office last night. Can you identify that intruder?"

Egorov shuffled his feet. "It was awfully dark," he said, trying to avoid the question.

"Egorov! Identify the intruder!"

Egorov took a long, hard look at Sydney. Sydney met his eyes. She was scared and helpless, every inch the pitiful farm girl in over her head. Tears ran down her face. Her skin and hair were nothing like those of the woman he'd encountered the night before.

Then he looked at Anna. Anna, who was wearing the black fatigues. Anna, who barked orders at all the men he worked with. After a few seconds of studying them, he raised his hand and pointed.

"Her. It was her."

He was pointing at Anna.

"What?" Anna exclaimed. "You little toad, how dare you accuse me—"

"Are you sure?" Voice Number One prompted.

Egorov took another look. If anything sent him over the top, it was Anna's last comment. "Yes. I'm positive."

"Thank you, Egorov, that will be all." Egorov gave a halfhearted salute and beat a hasty retreat.

A phone rang in the balcony. Voice Number Two answered. "Yes? . . . All right, send him in."

Leo shuffled in. He looked terrible. Dark circles hung under his eyes, and his normally stooped frame was even more hunched.

"Leo," Voice Number One said. "We're told you have evidence to present."

"I do," he replied, staring at Sydney. "Lower the screen, please."

A large projector screen descended to Sydney's right. "After the intruder's departure, we recovered a discarded phone from the premises." He produced Sydney's cell phone, which Shostok had found the night before. It was sealed in an evidence bag.

"Trapped in the earpiece was a hair. I ran a DNA test. We won't get the final results back for another forty-eight hours. However, from the random sampling I took, you'll notice the following. First slide, please."

The image showed two strands laid out side by side. Indentations marked different points on each strand. Sydney recognized them immediately as DNA strings laid out for comparison.

"The top sample is DNA from the hair," Leo explained. "The bottom is Petrova's, from her entrance application. You'll see that the DNA is not a match."

"So?" Anna said. "So what? It could be anybody's hair. That doesn't mean it's not her phone."

"No," Leo confirmed. "But I do have one other piece of information to show. Can you run the tape, please."

Surveillance footage of Sydney entering the building ran on a loop. She recognized herself, but anybody looking at the footage wouldn't be able to place her because of the hat that covered her features. And whoever it was had skin the same color as Anna's.

"The intruder was exceptionally skilled at dodging our cameras," Leo said. "It's likely she knew the position of each CCTV unit we have on sublevel seven. However, we did get one angle of her face."

The loop of Sydney walking through the halls was replaced by footage from Gregoran's office. The time code at the bottom read 2:13 A.M.

The woman onscreen stared straight at the camera. It was Anna.

Leo had done it. He had masked the footage.

She'd begged him to do it the night before, telling him exactly where she'd be at 2:12 A.M. It would be a five-second clip, just long enough for him to cut Anna's image off any of the hundreds of hours they had her on camera and paste it over Sydney's. And once he was successful, he should go to a certain bar the next day to be extracted.

Five seconds. It was long enough that anybody watching would definitely see Anna. But it was short enough that Leo could do the job in a night.

"This is a conspiracy!" Anna screamed. "You!" She whirled on Leo. "You've been tight with her all along! You and she, you're working together on this!"

"I just want to go home." Sydney sniffled. "I want to go home to the farm. I want to feed my cat, Demetria."

The comment was meant for Gregoran. Startled, he snapped a look at her. His face said it all: her *cat*? Demetria was her cat?

But Sydney just shook her head. "I don't understand why this is even happening. I'm loyal to K-Directorate. I would never sell it out. Can you find somebody else to persecute?"

Each word was a coded message for Gregoran, a reminder of the conversations they'd had since they met.

"You have to tell me everything you know about SD-9 so I can give K-Directorate somebody else to persecute."

"How do I know you're not going to sell me out the first moment you get?"

"A lot of people put their faith in Josef. You're going to have to put your faith in me."

Gregoran stared at her now with what could only be described as resigned respect. He had the air of a man who finally understood how completely he had been manipulated, who felt the despair that came with realizing he had only one option left, which was to burn all his bridges.

"I have something I'd like to add," Gregoran finally piped up. The rustling of bodies and the quiet whispering from the balcony hushed instantly.

"Agent Espinosa," Gregoran said, shaking his head, "has been working against us from the very beginning. She has spoken of trying to compromise this institution for her own gain. This is why I was unable to maintain a personal relationship with her."

Anna's face fell in that moment. "Pietr . . . ?" she asked, heartbroken.

"Why didn't you report her?" Voice Number Two asked.

"Because I loved her," Gregoran answered. "I didn't want to see her get hurt, and I thought I could control her. But this has gone too far. And it has to stop. Especially since she's trying to pin her crimes on an innocent young girl." He turned to Anna. "I'm sorry."

The stunned look stayed on Anna's face. She couldn't answer him. The sense of betrayal was so great that Sydney almost felt bad for her. But the feeling passed.

"We've heard enough," Voice Number One announced. "Release Petrova."

"No!" Anna screamed. "You can't tell me you believe this! Don't let her go!"

"Agent Espinosa," Voice Number Two warned, "you're in no position to give orders."

A troop of guards entered. Two of them released Sydney while the other four surrounded Anna. Sydney stood, but her legs were rubbery. Leo offered her support and she leaned on him gratefully and staggered out.

Behind her, she heard, "Agent Espinosa, you will be held here until we can complete a full investigation into your whereabouts last night!"

"This is a farce!" Anna's voice was cracking. "You're releasing the wrong woman!"

"Wait," Sydney whispered to Leo. "Turn me around." Leo obliged her, and Sydney stared at Anna one last time.

Anna stared back, daggers practically shooting out of her eyes. But Sydney wasn't scared of her anymore.

She held the look.

And then she smiled.

Gotcha.

*   *   *

Three hours later, Sydney stepped off a transit bus and crossed the street to the Screaming Boar. There had been a detail following her, but she'd lost them on the fourth double-back between K-Directorate and the bar. She felt that she'd mastered everything Diana had taught her. She'd stood out purposely from a crowd in the middle of a busy Moscow street—then she'd turned inward.

And like that, she'd disappeared.

She'd chuckled to herself as she watched the two-man team frantically comb the block trying to figure out where she'd gone. She'd disappeared down an alley, found the entrance to the subway, and taken a long way to the bar.

Now Sydney slipped inside, not attracting anyone's attention. She asked for the twelve-year-old scotch and sat down in the third booth from the bathroom.

Leo was already waiting for her.

"How did you get out?" she asked.

"Are you kidding?" he scoffed. "As soon as you left, Gregoran disappeared. Since his testimony was crucial in Anna's prosecution, K-Directorate is scouring Moscow looking for him. That man has a lot to answer for. They're not going to notice me stepping out for lunch and never returning. Even if I do have trouble going unnoticed under most circumstances."

"It will only be a matter of time before they figure out we lied to them," Sydney said. "Some forensics tech will notice you altered the security footage. Or they'll find one of my smudged fingerprints somewhere." Sydney leaned on the table, suddenly exhausted. "Not to mention that K-Directorate will be hunting for Sydney Bristow for a long time."

"They'll be hunting for Sasha Petrova," Leo corrected her.

"No, they'll be going after me."

"You did what you had to do in a crisis. No one can say you made a mistake."

The door opened and Sydney saw a grizzled man enter. He wouldn't have caught her attention, except that the lines under his eyes looked familiar. He was limping a little bit. And when he saw her, he smiled and she noticed he was missing some teeth.

He went to the bar, ordered a soda, and joined them in the booth. "Where'd they find you?" he asked Leo. "Reject for the *Jack and Beanstalk* auditions?"

"Leo," Sydney said, "meet Anatoly Gromnovich."

Gromnovich sat down with them in the booth. "This is Leo," Sydney said. "He's—"

"We know who he is."

"Who are *you*?" Leo asked.

"I'm your extraction," Gromnovich said with a crafty smile. "I'm the one who keeps you from having to crowd into the women's bathroom stall and wedge through a three-foot crawl space." He turned to Sydney. "The car's outside, but we have a few minutes. Here, I'll trade you."

Gromnovich took her scotch and gave her his soda. Then he raised his glass. "So. What are we drinking to?"

Leo raised his. "To getting out of there alive," he proposed.

Sydney raised hers. "And to those who didn't."

With that, they clinked glasses.

19

SLOANE SET DOWN THE papers. "Amazing."

The report, as she could tell by skimming notes upside down, was a summary of three debriefs she had given in transit back to Los Angeles. SD-9 had debriefed her fully before putting her on a plane. She'd been debriefed again on the flight across the Atlantic, and a third time at SD-6. By this point, she had gone over the story so many times, she knew exactly which details to highlight to absorb her questioners' interest.

Sloane could tell she'd been looking but didn't seem to mind. "You installed the virus on their system, you extracted yourself from that awful place—and you did it all in six days instead of six weeks. Not to mention we have a complete X-ray of K-Directorate's operational infrastructure—while ours is no longer at risk. Simply amazing."

"Thank you," Sydney said.

Noah leaned forward in his chair. He hadn't said anything to her since she'd arrived, but then he hadn't had a chance. The moment she had landed at LAX, she'd been transported immediately to a safe house, where she'd showered and changed clothes. From there, she had been taken to Credit Dauphine, where she'd been given a five-man escort to psych ops and, after that, to Sloane's office. She'd caught only glimpses of Noah in the hallways, and she had read the hungry look on his face. Not just a desire for a long, luxurious first kiss, but a need to reconnect. She knew him well enough to know that he wanted to hold her, to tell her how much he had missed her.

"Nobody's ever done what you've been able to do, Sydney," Noah said. "Not under those circumstances. Agents with five times your experience would have crumbled under that kind of pressure."

"You know," Sydney said looking down at her hands, "SD-6 thinks that I work best by myself in high-pressure scenarios. But the fact is, I had a lot of help. People who shouldn't have trusted me did. And people who had no reason to . . . sacrificed everything."

Every time she started thinking about Diana, tears sprang into her eyes. It was an uncontrollable response. She understood that it would fade in time. But, oddly, there was a part of her that didn't want it to. She wanted to get emotional when she thought of her Russian handler—and everything that Diana had done for her. If that was the only testament she could give, at least it meant that Diana wouldn't be forgotten.

"Is there anything we can offer you?" Sloane asked. "After a mission of this intensity, you've certainly earned SD-6's full appreciation. Which, as you know, is expansive."

Sydney had been thinking about this since she got on the plane. "I'd like the rest of the summer off."

Sloane nodded. "What else?"

"Nothing else. I just want my summer. What's left of it."

Sloane seemed taken aback by this. For a strange moment, Sydney almost thought he would say no because she hadn't asked for *more*. Instead, he said, "That can be arranged."

Sydney stood even though she hadn't been dismissed. "I'll see you in September."

Sloane smiled warmly. "I'm glad you're back, Sydney. You have no idea how worried we were. How much we all worked to make sure you got back safely."

Noah let his hand rest on her elbow. "I chewed out eight SD-9 agents alone for not extracting you. It's a wonder they'll still deal with us."

Sydney looked directly at Noah. There was no judgment, but there was a shift. His usual confidence and swagger disappeared in the blink of an eye.

Sydney didn't let him off the hook. Out of the corner of her eye, she could see Sloane folding his hands, almost delighted by the scene.

"We could have done more," Noah spluttered. "We *should* have."

Sydney wasn't entirely sure why Noah was talking like this. She hadn't accused him of anything. It wasn't until he'd stuck his foot in his mouth that she'd even doubted SD-6's intentions. Then, she realized that, without even noticing it, she was projecting the confidence that Diana had told her about. And it was making him nervous.

"I'm sure you did everything you could," Sydney said. She nodded good-bye to Sloane, turned, and walked out of the office, leaving Noah with his mouth still open.

She made it to the Credit Dauphine lobby before Noah caught up with her.

"What was *that* about?" he demanded.

"What?" Sydney asked. She didn't even slow down.

"In the office. I meant what I said. We were pulling for you."

"I know."

"Then why'd you have to act that way?"

Sydney turned to face him. "Noah, I'm tired and I want to go home. It's not all about you, okay?"

The same look of shock crossed his face, followed by indignation. But he sensed that he had to tread lightly. So he followed up with "Well, when do I get to see you again?"

Sydney turned her confidence on again. "I don't know. There's somebody else I have to see first."

"Somebody else?'

"Yes."

"Who?"

Sydney rolled her eyes. "For God's sake, I'm not cheating on you."

"Cheating? Who said cheating?"

"I did. Because you're acting weird. And the last thing I need is your fragile ego jumping to conclusions."

"Hey, I'm still not sure if we're having a relationship," Noah said, trying for nonchalantness and failing miserably. "Last time I checked, we were still *dating.*"

"Fine."

"Fine."

"Good."

"Good."

Sydney spun on her heel and walked out of the building. "So who *are* you seeing?" Noah called after her.

* * *

The gun rested in Sydney's lap as she sat on the bed. She'd made sure to pump it so that she wouldn't be caught off guard when she needed to fire.

She heard the door to her dorm open and slam. The jangling of keys and the rustling of plastic grocery bags. Francie entered, startled by an unexpected presence.

"Surprise!" Sydney said. She raised the Super Soaker water gun and pulled the trigger. The jet of water hit Francie square in the face. Francie immediately dropped the groceries that weighed down both hands and screamed.

The jet ended and Sydney started pumping the

water gun for another round. "Waitwaitwaitwait!" Francie cried. But simultaneously, Francie flew into the bathroom. Sydney chased her, thinking she could cut her roommate off. But Francie was crafty and quick. She slammed the bathroom door in Sydney's face before Sydney could soak her again.

"What are you *doing*?" Francie squealed, her voice ringing with delight.

"Well, right now the score is one–zip. I think I can get at least five more points on you."

She heard bathroom cabinets open and shut, and faucets from the sink and bathtub turn on. Francie was arming herself. "No," Francie said, "what are you doing back so soon?"

"The person running the internship was switched to a different position, so the program is on hiatus."

The faucets turned off. "When do you have to go back?"

"I don't. I get the whole summer off."

"The *whole* summer?"

"Yep."

Francie giggled. "Well, what do you want to do, then?"

"I don't know. I was thinking maybe we could go get some ice cream. Bike down the Promenade. Whatever you want."

"Sounds good to me."

Sydney got into position. "So why don't you come out and maybe we could start enjoying the summer for a change."

Sydney heard the lock on the other side of the door click. "You're on. Oh, and Sydney?"

"Yeah?"

The door flew open. Francie had two Super Soakers, one in each hand. "You're *dead*."